The Occult Files Of Francis Chard by AM Burrage

Alfred McLelland Burrage was born in Hillingdon, Middlesex on 1st July, 1889. His father and uncle were both writers, primarily of boy's fiction, and by age 16 AM Burrage had joined them. The young man had ambitions to write for the adult market too. The money was better and so was his writing.

From 1890 to 1914, prior to the mainstream appeal of cinema and radio the printed word, mainly in magazines, was the foremost mass entertainment. AM Burrage quickly became a master of the market publishing his stories regularly across a number of publications.

By the start of the Great War Burrage was well established but in 1916 he was conscripted to fight on the Western Front. He continued to write during these years documenting his experiences in the classic book War is War by Ex-Private X.

For the remainder of his life Burrage was rarely printed in book form but continued to write and be published on a prodigious scale in magazines and newspapers. In this volume we concentrate on his supernatural stories which are, by common consent, some of the best ever written. Succinct yet full of character each reveals a twist and a flavour that is unsettling.....sometimes menacing....always disturbing.

There are many other volumes available in this series together with a number of audiobooks. All are available from iTunes, Amazon and other fine digital stores.

Table Of Contents

The Hiding Hole
The Pit In The Garden
The Affair At Penbillo
The Third Visitation
The Woman With Three Eyes
The Soldier
The Tryst
The Bungalow At Shammerton
The Protector
The Girl In Blue
AM Burrage – The Life And Times

The Hiding Hole

Somebody brought young Adversain to the club, and Chard and I were introduced to him. I have had to disguise his family name, or you would know it well. The Adversains are one of the oldest houses in England, and through two hundred and fifty years of penal laws they adhered unfaltering to the Catholic tradition. There are three peerages in the family today, and there must be nearly enough money to finance a nation at war.

Young Francis Xavier Adversain was a nice shy boy of not more than twenty-two, fresh from Downside and Oxford. He played cricket for the M.C.C. and the Emeriti, and was well known at the Bath and the Bucks Clubs. He was obviously glad to meet Chard, and for a reason which he was soon to divulge.

'I've read some accounts of your experiences, Mr Chard,' he said, 'and I've been tremendously interested.'

Chard smiled.

'One-third of the world thinks me a crank,' he said, 'and another third thinks that—well, to put it mildly, that I've a pretty strong imagination.'

'I must belong to the third third,' laughed Francis Adversain.

'Thanks. I admit the peculiarity of my hobby, but apart from that I feel myself to be a normal and commonplace person. At least, I'm commonplace enough to feel like a whisky and soda. Won't you sit down and join us?'

Young Adversain's official host had faded away somewhere, and it was obvious to me, as it was to Chard, that the young man had been brought to the club specially to meet us. We had to ourselves a quiet comer of the Big Room, and I pulled three heavy armchairs within a sociable distance of one another. Chard called a waiter and gave an order, and, as we sat down, one of those uncomfortable silences ensued. We all seemed to discover simultaneously that, for the moment, we had nothing to say.

Chard was the first to speak. Turning to Adversain with a smile, he said,

'Well, won't you begin now?'

Adversain looked taken aback, and his eyes asked a question.

'I think,' Chard proceeded, 'that there was something you wanted to ask me. It was an impression I gathered. '

'Oh, yes! Yes! It was about our ghost at home. We have a ghost, you know. At least, I don't know what else to call it. Or, to be a little less vague, there's one perfectly good bedroom which we can't use. I wonder if you'd be kind enough to give me some advice '

'I shall be delighted, if you'll give me some particulars.'

The young man leaned back and narrowed his brows.

'It will probably seem very trivial to you,' he said; 'in fact, it seems trivial to us, but it's puzzling and unaccountable. We've all of us tackled that room, and sometimes put guests in it, and everyone's had the same experience. One wakes in the night, literally stifling. I don't mean hot, but unable to breathe. There is no air in that room at all, or, rather, one can't breathe it, even with all the windows wide open. It may strike you as foolish to rush to the supernatural for an explanation, but what other explanation can there be?'

'An old house?' Chard asked.

'Yes, early Tudor. Gillingdean Hall'

'Ah,' said Chard, 'of course I've heard of it. It was a famous house in the late sixteenth and early seventeenth centuries. In fact, I seem to remember that it sheltered two men connected with the Gunpowder Plot.'

'The alleged Gunpowder Plot,' Adversain corrected, with a faint smile. 'In those days it was the seat of the Gillingtons. They are now extinct, and the property came to us through a Miss Gillington, the last of the family, who married an ancestor of mine. The Gillingtons, like ourselves, had always been Catholics, and old Lady Mary Gillington, who lived there at the time you have mentioned, had been a Catesby before her marriage. I don't know if you are fond of old houses, Mr Chard?'

'Very.'

'Then ours would amuse you. We've already found seven secret hiding-places. The Gillingtons had Mass said there every Sunday in defiance of the law, and many a priest owes his life to Nicholas Owen, who came down and constructed these hiding-places for them.'

'That,' said Chard, 'was the Jesuit who used to be called Little John. They caught him at last and tortured him to death in the Tower, but he gave nothing away. Nearly every hiding-hole in old country houses is the work of Little John.'

'You know as much about it as I do, Mr Chard,' Adversain laughed.

'What worries us more than the room which we can't use is the fact that there's a secret exit from the house, and we can't find it. If there's a secret exit there must also be a secret entrance, and anybody who happened to stumble across the other end could enter the house at will.'

'Rather awkward,' I laughed. 'But are you sure it exists?'

'We know that it did exist, because of the story of Father Mead on the day Lady Mary Gillington died. Would it interest you to hear?'

'Thanks,' said Chard. 'Very much.'

'Well, in the bad old times, early in the seventeenth century, there was a room at the house used as a chapel, and Mass was celebrated there whenever a priest came round. Lady Mary Gillington used to order the house-linen to be hung on a certain hedge on these occasions, so that all those who belonged to the Old Faith might know that there was a priest at the house and they could come there and hear Mass. Father Mead was a Jesuit who went around from one Catholic Hall to another, disguised as a travelling musician who gave lessons in the virginals. The pursuivants, or priest-hunters, knew quite well what was going on, but they could never catch their man. They came nearest to it on the day when Lady Mary Gillington died.

'This was on a Sunday. The linen was out on the hedge, and Father Mead was saying Mass, when the pursuivants suddenly raided the house. The candles were snuffed out and everything was safely hidden away. Only old Lady Mary knew the secrets of the house, and she hustled Father Mead away, nobody knew whither. But the pursuivants were not to be put off. They could smell the snuffed-out candles, and knew what had been going on. Old Lady Mary Gillington began to harangue them indignantly, and suddenly fell down in a seizure and died. She was the only person in the house who knew its secrets, and thus might have been made to speak, and her sudden death must have been a blow to the unwelcome visitors.

'They stayed in the house for more than a week, watching everybody, so that none could have brought food to Father Mead, even if they had known where he was hidden. At the end of a week it began to dawn on them that there must be some secret exit from the house, that their quarry had long since got safely away, and that they were wasting their time. That is how we know that there is, or was, a secret exit.'

'And what happened to Father Mead?'

Young Adversain shrugged his shoulders.

'History does not relate. I suppose, poor wretch, he was caught on some subsequent occasion and hanged, drawn and quartered like most of the others. '

Chard nodded absently.

'To return to the room which you can't use,' he said, 'is there any story in your family to account for it?'

'None that I know of. The room's always been like that. Nobody's worried about it, except that just now and again somebody tries the experiment of sleeping there, always with the same result. One has to leg it out of that room pretty quick and get a breath of air on the other side of the threshold. Of course, my people won't have anything done that smacks of spiritualism, and exorcism seems rather drastic for something which we only vaguely attribute to the supernatural. But I've often thought we ought to take serious notice of it. It may be a signal from some poor departed soul which still wants human aid.'

Chard glanced at me. 'I should like to see that room,' he said.

Adversain smiled.

'I was hoping you'd suggest it. We should be so grateful if you'd come down for a weekend. When would it be convenient?'

'Almost any weekend.'

Adversain considered and then glanced in a note-book.

'You don't want to run into a huge crowd on an affair of this sort?' he said. 'Do you think I could borrow the telephone here for a trunk call? I'll ring up home and see what's happening next weekend. Or would that be too early for you? I thought of week-ending at home.'

So I took young Adversain downstairs and handed him over to the hall-porter, who put his call through for him. When he emerged from the box he said to me what he subsequently said to Chard.

'My father and mother will be away for the weekend. If you care to come down with me there will be only ourselves and Father Stevens, the chaplain.

Or will that be too dull for you?'

'It will be excellent,' Chard answered. 'It may sound ungracious, but the fewer people about on an occasion of this sort the better. Mind, I can't promise to make any definite discoveries. I can only do my best.'

Neither Chard nor I was unduly excited over the prospective adventure. A room in which one was sometimes unable to breathe seemed not to promise any great excitement. But Gillingdean Hall was an extremely interesting house, and for that reason we welcomed the opportunity of visiting it.

The house is in Berkshire, some fifteen miles west of Reading. It is reached by a bye-road, and so screened by trees that hundreds who have passed through that countryside must be unaware of its existence. It is built of red brick, now mellowed to an autumn tint, and contains some of the finest carved oak in England. Nearly all the rooms are panelled, and one saw everywhere the rose of the House of Tudor.

Young Adversain drove us down and introduced us to Father Stevens.

The Adversains maintain the tradition of keeping a resident chaplain. There is a little chapel nowadays under the lee of the great house, where the Catholics on the estate worship every day, or at least every week.

Father Stevens was a charming man and a broad-minded, but his face fell a little when he heard the object of our visit. However, it cleared when we told him that we were not spiritualists, and disliked the cult almost as much as he too disliked it.

'About the room,' he said, 'I simply don't account for it. I have slept there—or tried to sleep there—and met the same fate as the other experimentalists. It may be that some poor soul in purgatory is trying to attract attention. I will say Mass for him, or her, tomorrow morning.'

'And I'll have a shot at sleeping in that room tonight, if I may,' said Chard.

We were shown the room. It was in the front of the house, looking straight across the park through a narrow cutting in the trees, and for size and position it was one of the best rooms in the house. Except that a modem and comfortable bed had been placed in it, and a thick carpet covered the floor, it must have been very much as it was in the days of Lady Mary Gillington. There was an open hearth, in which a small grate had been set without altering the structure or spoiling its appearance. I was given the next room, and Chard was provided with a secondary bedchamber further down the passage. 'Because,' said Adversain, 'he's certain to be driven out in the night.'

Before dinner Adversain showed us over the house and revealed half a dozen secret hiding-places. The house seemed to be honeycombed with them, and still paid tribute to the ingenuity of 'Little John'. An attic stair could be removed bodily, revealing a cavity underneath. An innocent-looking cupboard masked the entrance to another cupboard. A window-seat lifted up and revealed a dark and narrow chamber underneath. The old mechanisms still worked admirably after more than three hundred years.

These hiding-holes were hard enough to discover when they were empty.

When occupied they must have provided the refugee with safety almost proportionate to the discomfort he had to endure. There was a wooden bolt on the inside of each, so that even if the seekers stumbled across the secret mechanism the door remained fast.

We dined at eight and, after three or four rubbers of shilling bridge, went early to bed.

It must have been between twelve and one when I was wakened by the sound of the door next to mine crashing open. I jumped out of bed, threw open my own door and looked out—to behold Chard on the landing in his pyjamas, gasping for breath and laughing.

'It's true about that infernal room,' he said, when he was partly recovered. 'I can't breathe in it, or I couldn't just now. It was like being in a vacuum. I woke fighting for breath. Both my windows wide open, too. I wonder what on earth it means.'

'Let me try,' I said.

I went in, and, after half a minute, I came out again, drawing breath as if I had just come up to the surface after a deep dive. There was no sensation of horror such as I had previously suffered in 'haunted' rooms, nothing but the simple inability to draw breath. The thing was inexplicable. Chard came into my room, borrowed my dressing-gown, and sat on my bed talking for a little while.

'What do you make of it?' I asked.

'I don't know. But I'm on the track of an idea. People who sleep in that room get the sensations of somebody who once slept in it perhaps hundreds of years ago. It may be automatic, or there may be a mind at work. Somebody no longer of this world is trying to attract our attention.'

'You think that somebody was once stifled to death in that room?'

'I do. Whether he or she was smothered while in bed I can't say. But if some spirit is trying to tell us something and we go half-way to meet it we shall probably learn a great deal more. By the way, ever played that "willing" game? Somebody goes out of the room, and when he comes back everybody present wills him to do something which, if he is successful in keeping his mind blank, he generally does?'

'Yes, I've played it,' I answered, smiling, 'but I'm not a very good subject.'

'Nor am I,' said Chard. 'But I wonder if Adversain or the padre are any good.'

He asked the same question at the breakfast table. Father Stevens was not present, having to fast until he had said his second Mass.

'As a matter of fact,' said Adversain, 'we play that game quite a lot, and Father Stevens is very good indeed.'

'Splendid!' said Chard enthusiastically. 'What time will he be free?' Adversain considered

'Second Mass is at eleven o'clock. It's a low Mass, and won't take long. Then he'll say his Thanksgiving and have a snack to last him over to lunch time. I should think he'll be free about a quarter-past twelve. Why do you want him?'

'I want him to play that game in the room I got driven out of last night.'

'He won't if he thinks it's encroaching on spiritualism.'

'Well, it won't be. I just want him to keep his mind a blank, and I want you and Torrance not to will at all. Something else has got to do the willing.

All we've got to do is just watch what he does.'

But it took Chard some ten minutes to overcome the good Father's scruples.

'I am convinced, Father Stevens,' said Chard, 'that some poor spirit wants to tell us something. We are not calling up spirits or any dangerous nonsense of that sort, but just lending our ears to one who is trying to call us—a good spirit, I am convinced. Surely it is our duty to help it if we can.'

So at about half an hour after noon we went upstairs, all four, into that room in which all who had slept awoke stifling. The strong sunlight was pouring in, and nothing could have been less eerie than the atmosphere in which we made our experiment. Father Stevens stood in the middle of the room, and we other three sat on the bed. The priest faced us, and his eyes were open, but after a minute or two I saw a glaze come over them. Then he turned slowly and faced the fireplace.

We could still see his face in profile, and remarked a sudden contortion of his features. His hands went to his throat like a man fighting for breath.

Then, slowly, one step at a time, he walked towards the hearth.

We all three got up and followed him softly. Right in the arch of the fireplace he paused, hesitated a moment, and then reached up with his hand and tapped a blackened beam inside the chimney. Then he turned to us with a smile and dropped his hands.

'That was what I felt impelled to do,' he said. 'Were you willing me?'

But none of us answered him Adversain was already in the hearth and looking up the chimney with a lighted match in his hands. The chimney was built of brick and beam.

'There are two bricks missing,' he said.

'Yes,' said Chard simply, 'to give air. And what lets in air will let in smoke. '

Adversain turned swiftly to Chard.

'What do you mean?' he asked bluntly.

'There's another secret chamber up there—one you knew nothing about. I don't know where the entrance is, but you'd better not waste time. Let's get a crowbar and knock those bricks away. I think you'll find inside the bones of a Christian who wants Christian burial.'

'The bones? Whose bones?' We were all staring at Chard.

'Father Mead's—unless I'm very much deceived. They've been there for more than three hundred years. And there's no secret exit from your house, Mr Adversain. There never was. It was only assumed that there was because the pursuivants remained in the house for a week without finding the poor priest. After Lady Mary died suddenly nobody knew where he was hidden.'

Father Stevens and young Adversain both turned upon Chard faces which were blank with astonishment.

'And you mean he stayed there and starved to death?'

'No, I don't. Somebody, not knowing where he was, lit a fire, and he was stifled by the smoke. He has been trying, in the only way possible to him, to tell people ever since. I may be wrong, of course, but that's my theory. It's the only one I can find to fit. And if there is a secret chamber in that chimney, and we find a man's skeleton in it, I shall be perfectly satisfied.'

'I'll go and get a crowbar,' said Adversain, through his teeth.

And so it happened that a carpenter on the estate was mystified at receiving an order for a coffin, without having heard of any death. We did not trouble the coroner with the poor bones which we found in a narrow space behind the back of the chimney. We ourselves dug the martyr's grave in the shadow of the chapel wall, and Father Stevens read the burial service over it.

Young Adversain now sleeps in the room in which once it was impossible to sleep. He says it is the most comfortable in the house.

The Pit in the Garden

Francis Chard occasionally wrote short articles dealing with his experiences of the supernormal, and his less abstruse and, therefore, more popular effusions were generally printed in the Sunday papers. These hardly ever failed to produce a mixed bag of letters from strangers, which were in due time re-addressed to him, subsequently to provide us with a certain amount of entertainment.

Most of these letters came from sceptics or hardened materialists, and varied in tone between gentle chaff and vulgar abuse. Prosy old gentlemen whose mental balances were plainly precarious expounded their own theories in long, closely-written pages. There were the usual touting letters from professional clairvoyants. And occasionally there came a communication which was interesting and which had to be taken seriously. One such arrived on a certain Monday evening in October, having been written and posted on the Sunday evening, and re-directed from the newspaper office that same day. Chard brought it round to show it to me, and I read as follows:

Hie Oak Inn,
Blakebury Common,

Berks, Oct. 8, 1925

Dear Sir,

My wife and I have read with much interest your article in today's Weekly Standard, and I am writing to ask if perhaps you could help us. We don't exactly believe in ghosts, but funny things happen here sometimes, and during the last week we've been scared out of our wits. We've never taken much notice before, but just this last week it's been dreadful. I'm not much of a hand at letter-writing, so I won't try to explain what's been going on; but my wife and I both thought you might be interested to come down and see for yourself, and then if you could tell us what to do to stop what's been happening we should both be much obliged to you and truly grateful.

Hoping you can come

Yours faithfully,

G. HAMLIN PARKER

'What do you think of that?' Chard inquired, as I folded up the letter to replace it in its envelope.

'It's intriguing,' I said, 'because he really doesn't tell you anything. Probably if he'd said what had been happening one wouldn't be quite so interested.'

'It rather looks as if a variety of things have been happening, and our friend the landlord feels incapable of describing them adequately. I shouldn't say that he's an imaginative man. Although he's quite obviously distressed by the mysterious "things" which have been happening, he still won't admit that he believes in ghosts. I think I shall go down tomorrow. Blakebury Common is only about fifty miles out of London, and if it's a false alarm I shan't have wasted very much time. Coming?'

I said that I would be glad to accompany him. I had no engagement until the Wednesday evening, and that I was very willing to cancel if genuine and interesting phenomena were to be experienced at the Oak Inn.

Chard accordingly wired to the landlord on the following morning, and after lunch we set out for Berkshire together in his car.

The Bath Road took us as far as Reading, where the map told us to branch off on to a road which passed through Bradfield and on through a lonely, sparsely populated countryside to the desolation of the grassy, wind-haunted downs. We stopped in Reading for a few minutes, where, on finding that Blakebury Common had a guide-book all to itself, purchased a copy, and read it while Chard drove the car. We had already passed Eastfield Cottage before I found a reference to the Oak Inn, and it was so interesting that I made him stop the car and read it for himself.

'On the south side of the Common, about a mile from Blakebury village, stands the Oak Inn, a favourite meeting-place of the West Berks Foxhounds. The inn has been modernised, but parts of it are very ancient and tradition says that two of Queen Elizabeth's henchmen were lodged there upon the occasion of her Majesty's state visit to Blakebury Hall. Despite this Royal patronage, however, the inn seems to have had a bad reputation during the 17th and

18th centuries. It was a notorious resort of highwaymen, and more than one lonely traveller who mysteriously disappeared was last seen in the vicinity of the Oak Inn.'

Chard read the passage and smiled.

'Romantic,' he said, 'and suggestive. But I don't suppose the trouble there—if there is any trouble—originated in those days. I've investigated so many phenomena in old houses in which one would naturally look to the remote past for the cause, only to find that the disturbances were due to some comparatively recent happening. Still, I'm glad you picked up this guide.'

Half-an-hour later, and only so late as that because we lost our way, we arrived at the Oak Inn. The Parkers were used to motorists stopping there but they seemed to recognise us instinctively when we pulled up. The landlord came out to greet us and directed us to the garage at the back. He was rather well dressed, youngish, and fresh-faced, and we were soon to learn that he had lately worked in a city office. War service had whetted his appetite for a freer life in the country, and a temporary failing of health had led to his abandoning the safe and dull job for the more speculative career of country innkeeper. I took particular notice of him while he guided us round and threw open the door of a great roomy shed, to which we made our way slowly, scattering chickens and ducks to left and right. He was not at all the type of man to be martyred by his imagination.

Mrs Parker, whom we met inside the house a minute or two later, looked a year or two younger than her husband. She was a quiet, kindly, blue-eyed woman, who showed symptoms of nervous strain. There were reasons for this, as we discovered later.

'It's very good of you to come,' she said to us. 'I've lit a fire in the sitting room upstairs, and I can show you your bedrooms. I've laid tea, and the kettle's on for our own, so I shan't have to keep you waiting.'

Chard thanked her for both of us.

'But couldn't we have tea with you?' he asked. 'Then, at the same time we could hear all the details about what's been troubling you.'

'If you don't mind the kitchen' she began.

We neither of us did, and she led the way into the kitchen at the back of the public part of the house.

I must describe the ground floor of the inn. While the facade was ugly and modem, and there were signs in the interior of those so-called improvements which are dear to the hearts of the licensed trade, there were many evidences of antiquity. The house was larger than the average wayside inn, and somewhat intricately planned.

The one entrance in the front, the only public entrance, gave access to a passage, with a door leading into the large taproom on the right. On the left was a large room which went the whole length of the house, and two doors on that side of the passage both led into it. Farther down on the right hand side was another door flanked by windows, where a comer of the taproom had been partitioned off, and in which glasses, bottles, and barrels were kept, so that customers could be served both in the passage and in the taproom.

Beyond this enclosure, the passage took a turn to the right, with the kitchen and then the scullery on the left and, on the right once more, the stairs. We learned that the long room with the two doors on the left of the passage as we entered it was called the Club Room.

The kitchen was a good-sized and pleasant room, in which a cheerful fire was burning, and the window overlooked the yard behind and the shed in which Chard's car had been garaged. A large smooth-haired, black and white dog, of indeterminate breed, got off a horsehair chair to welcome us, and, having awakened to the probable imminence of food, flopped excitedly about the room, lashing chair-legs and the dresser cupboard with a tail like half a yard of whalebone. Parker came in and quieted him with a chunk of bread, made him go back to his chair, and lingered over him for a moment or two stroking his back.

'Bob's a good dog,' he said, 'and he looks after his missus.'

Then we all sat down around the table, and had tea, and gradually Chard and I discovered the reasons for the letter which had brought us there. I shall use the Parkers' own words as much as possible, but it would be too long and too tedious to tell their story exactly as I heard it. There was a great deal of repetition, and there were many interruptions.

You see, the Parkers clung to their disbelief as ardently as many disillusioned spiritualists cling to their faith. I have noticed that most people who believe in ghosts are either highly educated or woefully ignorant. The Parkers were town-bred, educated in practical and efficient schools, and brought up not to speculate on things which did not seem intimately to concern them. You know these people who are the backbone of the nation and the despair of the highbrows? Life to them is a journey from the cradle to the grave, with nothing beyond the last earthly stage, and money the motive power and lubrication which makes the journey smooth or otherwise.

They don't go to church, and seldom make themselves uncomfortable by thinking of the Unknown God, Whose existence most of them will grudgingly admit. They respect a recognised science because it is called a science, and not a superstition. Twenty-five years ago they would have smiled in your face and laughed behind your back for prophesying the marvels which have since been accomplished by wireless. Oh, yes, they would have, bless them!

To the Parkers, therefore, a ghost was something which didn't exist, and which was supposed to frighten people by walking about in a sheet. If you saw one you were either tipsy or required medical care. Nobody had been walking about the inn in a sheet, so it couldn't be a ghost, but something 'funny' and alarming had been happening, and so

Well, we got it out of Parker to begin with.

'We've been here four years,' he said, 'and we heard the house was supposed to be haunted before we came. Of course, we didn't believe in it, and took no notice. I suppose half-a-dozen queer things happened at night before the beginning of last week. We've thought we heard somebody walking about the house long after it was locked up, and we were all in bed, and I've gone down and there hasn't been a soul.

'Once one night we both woke up together, and we both thought we saw a face looking at us over the side of the bed. A big, fat white face it was, and one of the eyes squinted I expect one of us dreamed it, and the other imagined it through telepathy. Telepathy's recognised by scientists, isn't it? Anyhow, I jumped out of bed and lit a candle, and there was nothing there.

'And then we had Mr Smadley, the writer, and his wife, staying with us. They woke up one night and heard somebody trying to bash open the door of their room, and he jumped out of bed and found nothing there.'

'Tell them about Dick,' interpolated Mrs Parker.

'Oh, yes, Dick. That was a Mr Spring we had staying with us about a year ago.' Parker paused and spluttered joyously. 'Mr Spring wasn't a teetotaller, so we didn't take much notice of him. One night when the bar was closed, I was out washing glasses in the bar, and Mr Spring was standing in the passage having a whisky. Suddenly he went white and began pointing with his finger. "Look, look, look!" he said. We did look, but from what I could understand afterwards I must have been looking the wrong way.

He said he saw something like a blue shadow in the shape of a man come out through the club-room door opposite and go down the passage. But I didn't take much notice of that. He was entitled to see things. Oh, yes, we saw plenty of queer things happen before last Monday, but that's not gloss. Since then we've had rather a time of it.'

'What's been happening since then?' Chard asked.

Parker hesitated, and his wife prompted him.

'There was Mr McIver,' she said.

'Yes,' Parker continued, 'there was Mr McIver. I'd arranged for a petrol pump to be installed here. I get lots of inquiries for petrol—and Mr McIver was the engineer sent to supervise the job. He was to stay in the house one or two nights, but he only stayed the one, and said he'd be shot before he stayed another. Now nobody could say he'd been drinking. He hadn't had more than two half-pints of bitter. Well, after I'd shut up the house at ten o'clock, Mr McIver very kindly came and helped me with the glasses, while the wife went to get supper for all three of us. The brewers were coming next day and I had it in my mind that I was short of whisky, so I left Mr McIver for a minute and went down the cellar to see how my stock was. When I came back he was lying on the floor of the passage in a kind of faint.

'I brought him round, and then he swore that somebody had attacked him from behind, and he complained of a violent pain between the shoulder-blades. I thought he'd had some sort of fit and helped him to bed. Next morning he asked us who'd been walking about the house all night, and who was the man with the ugly white face and the squint who kept on looking into his room? And next night—well, you'd better tell them about next night, Dolly.'

Mrs Parker flinched a little at the suggestion.

'Yes,' she said, 'that was awful. Mr Parker has a way of falling asleep in the chair after supper, and once he's in bed he's asleep before his head strikes the pillow, as the saying is. Well, last Tuesday, a week ago tonight, we'd finished supper and he'd fallen asleep in his chair. After a time he woke up, asked me to do the locking-up, and went straight upstairs Not many minutes later I lit a candle and went round.

'The front door was already locked, but there was an iron bar to be put up. I attended to that first. I then locked the tap-room and the two club-room doors, and was turning to lock up the door leading to the bar when it happened. Old Bob was lying asleep on the mat. I'd just spoken to him and he'd flopped his tail at hearing my voice.

'Well, my back was towards the passage, and I was holding the candle in my left hand when I heard a noise as if the locked door of the club-room behind me was opening. I suddenly found myself in a dreadful state of fear, the candlestick was knocked out of my hand, and I felt myself being held by a—by a sort of force against the door of the bar. At the same moment I felt a most dreadful pain between my shoulders.

'Simultaneously Bob went mad. He jumped off his mat and went for—for something like a tiger. He was worrying and snarling and snapping all round my heels. Presently I felt myself released, and the dog went all down the passage by the wall, snarling and biting at something that wasn't there. I could hear the clash of his teeth coming together all the time.

'The noise of the dog woke Mr Parker, and he came running downstairs as I went running up. I was nearly fainting, but I managed to tell him something of what head been happening. He went all over the house, and found it locked up as I'd left it, and empty except for ourselves.'

Parker took up the tale again.

'Since then,' he said, 'we haven't had a night's peace. Bob won't sleep downstairs, and come and whines to be let into our room. We've seen that white face again, looking at us through our bedroom door. The dog saw it too and went nearly frantic. And there are noises all over the house all night, like people walking about in big boots. We don't believe in ghosts, either of us, but there's something funny going on, and having read your article, Mr Chard, we thought there could be no harm in writing to you.'

Chard and I exchanged looks.

'I'm very glad you did,' he said. 'All this sounds very interesting to me.'

He proceeded to ask a few questions, the answers to which left neither of us the wiser.

'Well,' he remarked at last, 'we shan't be able to do very much until after dark. Would you care for a quiet drive around the countryside in the car, Torrance? I think, Mr Parker, I should like a little juice from that new petrol pump of yours which, by the way, I didn't notice.'

'I can let you have a can,' the landlord replied, 'but the pump isn't up yet. The man had no sooner started digging the pit under Mr McIver's directions than an inspector arrived and insisted that we had the pump cemented in. I'm not going to pay for cement, and unless the firm that's contracted to supply the pump will pay for the cement I shan't have it at all.

They're still arguing about it with me.'

Chard smiled.

'Very well,' he said, 'we'll take a tin, and thank you very much.'

A few minutes later we walked out through the front door of the house, and Parker followed us. He pointed to a shallow oblong pit in the far comer of the garden.

'That's where the pump's going to be, if we have it at all,' he said. He saw us away in the car, having first listened to our promises to be back early.

'Just one favour I'd like to ask,' he said. 'Please don't tell anybody why you're here, or we shall have people laughing at us. If you should speak to any of the customers tonight, you're just two gentlemen staying on the road for the night.'

We duly pledged ourselves to this secrecy, and Chard drove us into Newbury, and thence straight along the Bath Road to Hungerford, where we took an early dinner. He said very little about the matter in hand except that in his opinion we had better be prepared for an unquiet night.

'What do you think of it all?' I asked him.

He shrugged his shoulders and smiled.

'I don't know yet,' he replied, 'but there's one circumstance seems to me extremely interesting. While there would seem always to be mild disturbances going on intermittently in that house, they have only become regular and violent since last Monday week. And you know what happened last Monday week?'

He had me guessing for the moment.

'No?' I said. 'What did happen last Monday week?'

'Somebody started digging a pit in a certain part of the garden. Doesn't it occur to you that it's rather a coincidence, and that if the digging operations had been continued something interesting might have been found? But we can look into that tomorrow.'

We were back at the Oak Inn by nine o'clock. There was no inn in Blakebury village about a mile away, which may have accounted for the business done by our host. The frequenters seemed mainly to be farm hands and builders' labourers, with a sprinkling of small farmers and dealers. The village Socialist was already drunk, and conducting a noisy argument with the Tory schoolmaster. Everything was normal until, at ten o'clock, the law compelled Parker to be inhospitable, and a representative of the law arrived outside to make sure that he was.

Chard and I disdained our upstairs sitting-room, and sat in the kitchen with the Parkers while they had their supper. At eleven o'clock Chard somewhat surprised them by announcing his intention of going to bed.

'If anything's happening,' he said, 'we shall be sure to hear it.'

Our rooms faced each other across a square landing. I meant to stay awake, but I don't think I stayed awake long. Nor, I think, was I long asleep. I was awakened by somebody walking boldly across by the foot of my bed to the door. The window on my left filtered the light of a bright, clear sky of stars, but I saw nothing. Nor did the door open as the footsteps seemed to cross my threshold. I sprang up myself, sweating, and flung it open.

At the same moment Chard's door on the other side of the landing flew open.

'You haven't been in my room?' he asked.

'I was just going to ask you the same thing,' I said, shakily.

He turned back into his room.

'Come along,' he said, 'we may as well take a look downstairs.'

We had each of us packed a dressing-gown and slippers, but I took longer to get into mine, and he did not wait for me. I took the precaution first to light a candle, and crept downstairs through an avenue of swelling and dwindling shadows. At the foot of the stairs I called out softly, 'Chard'.

I was answered by a queer strangled cry, which came from the passage leading to the door, and I hurried around the comer to pull myself up with a jerk, for I had nearly cannoned into a figure.

Only it wasn't Chard's figure. Chard was pressed against the door of the bar, immobile save for his face, which worked horribly. The figure into which I had nearly walked was towering over him, and I saw the flash of a long knife. Then I suppose I lost my head, for I flung the candlestick at it, plunging us all in darkness, and stumbled against Chard, who clung to me for a moment with the grip of a madman.

'It's gone now,' he said, thickly, after a moment. 'Oh, my God! My back!'

We got upstairs somehow, and I decided to bivouac for the rest of the night in Chard's room. I had seldom seen Chard so shaken.

'He knifed somebody in that passage one night, as he knifed me tonight,'

Chard muttered.

'Whom do you mean?' I stammered.

'How do I know? Some former landlord, I suppose. Perhaps it happened hundreds of years ago. I felt it go right through me, although I daresay there isn't a mark on my back.'

I looked for him, and there was nothing to see. There was some comfort in this, but not enough to allow either of us to sleep. Indeed, we made no attempt until the first light of morning came, when I returned to my own room. But first I left a pencilled message on the landing, asking the Parkers not to wake us.

It must have been half past eleven before I woke up, and when I opened my eyes Parker was in the room.

'I hope I haven't disturbed you,' he said, 'but something funny's happened.'

I stared at him and blinked. So far as I was concerned, I felt that the Oak Inn had exhausted all its possibilities of 'fun'.

'I fixed it up about the petrol pump this morning,' Parker continued, 'and the man went on digging the pit. And what do you think he found! A long, rusty, beastly-looking knife in the middle of a pile of human bones!' 'I thought it was something like that,' said Chard to me later in the day. 'It doesn't take much imagination to suppose that a spirit, compelled to haunt the scene of its crime, and in some measure re-enact it, would be stirred to greater activity at the prospect of that crime being brought to light. It was quite sufficient when they began to dig the earth above those bones. And it rather shows, doesn't it, that the country inns of the good old times weren't always what G.K. Chesterton would like us to believe? Well, I think things will quiet down now.'

And they did. Nobody at the Oak Inn has since been disturbed. The Parkers were very grateful to Chard for coming down, and they still maintain that something 'funny' used to happen sometimes. But they still don't believe in ghosts.

The Affair at Penbillo

I happened to be in Chard's company when Mr Leslie Traske called. Chard and I had just finished lunch and were sitting smoking over our coffee close by the great middle window of his dining-room, which overlooked a stretch of the embankment at Chelsea, a reach of the river, and the green grass and trees of Battersea Park.

It was due to a mistake on the part of the faithful Roberts that Traske was ushered into the dining-room. When Chard said, 'Show him up,' he meant that the visitor should be shown into the small, sedate-looking room, so like a doctor's consulting-room, in which he had received strangers since strangers had taken to calling on him. While Chard and I were idly wondering who this Mr Traske might be, and what he might want, the man himself was precipitated into our presence.

'Mr Chard?' he said as we both rose; and a true instinct brought him to rest his gaze on Chard, who acknowledged his identity with an inclination of the head 'I must apologise,' he continued, hastily and nervously, 'for coming to call on you without any warning. I meant to write to you—indeed, I did write—but when I left my Cornish home last night I found that the last mail had gone, and that if I were to see you before the evening my arrival would necessarily precede the letter.'

He was voluble and yet precise in his speech, and he looked nervously and apologetically at each of us in turn, with quick nods and little bird-like jerks of the head. He was a man of about sixty, and his clothes were eloquent of the retirement in which he normally lived. Although they were carelessly put on and were of a fashion some fifteen years old, they looked as if they had hardly been worn. I can see him now, a tall, colourless, lean man, with loose, flabby checks and hollow, anxious eyes. He had the stoop of a scholar, the accent of a gentleman, and the general air of a recluse. Chard laid his hand invitingly on the back of one of the chairs in the window.

'Won't you sit down, Mr Traske?' he asked. 'You must be tired after your long journey. I suppose you came up by the night train?'

'Yes. I arrived at Paddington at about eight o'clock this morning. This is my first visit to London for twenty years, and I hardly recognise it. I do so miss the hansoms and the old horse-buses. After some breakfast and a bath I have been spending my time walking about. Although I came up with no other object but to see you, Mr Chard, I confess I have been in two minds all the morning as to whether I could after all trespass on your time and patience. Now that I am more than three hundred miles distant from my home I can almost bring myself to believe that I have been the victim of my imagination, that my nerves have been playing me tricks. Indeed, when you have heard me, you are more than likely to ascribe my trouble to some kind of nervous disorder. I have no more to tell you—so far as mere words go—than an ordinary man would dismiss with a shrug of the shoulders. It was only the thought of returning home, and the realisation that I dared not return alone, which finally brought me to seek your help.'

I was rather awkwardly placed. Mr Traske had come to see Chard and not me, and ordinarily I should have retired and left them alone together. However, I knew that my presence was not unwelcome to Chard, whose intimate friend and confidant I was, and whose chronicler I now am; and the visitor, by addressing half his remarks to me, seemed anxious that I, too, should hear all he had to say. Chard clinched the matter by introducing me as his friend Torrance, and adding that I had assisted him in several of his investigations of psychic phenomena.

'Hardly that,' I confessed, smiling. 'I merely play Boswell to his Johnson.'

'Then you are to be envied in your association, Mr Torrance,' said Traske warmly. 'I live right out of the world, but I read a great deal, and I took a great deal of sympathetic interest in Mr Chard before ever I dreamed that I might need his services. It was refreshing to hear of a man who, although apparently well aware that spirit manifestations could, and did, take place, approached every individual case with the cautious step of the complete sceptic. I thought that here was a man upon whom the mantle of Podmore had fallen. But for you, Mr Chard, there is no serious investigation today. The others have long since disdained science, and are content to dwell on the threshold of the ridiculous fairy-land they have created for themselves. I have no patience with their earthly paradises, where it seems one must endure an even more vulgar and material kind of existence than this earth-life. If their tales are true there is no reason at all for living, and certainly none for dying. And, if I may say so, I like your plain way of writing, Mr Chard. You don't use the jargon I have come so to mistrust; you call a ghost a ghost.'

Chard smiled at that.

'After all,' he said, 'words are only words. I go to the dictionary for mine, and I prefer the simplest I can find. As to being a sceptic, I can assure you that I am always a sceptic as regards individual cases until I have assured myself one way or the other. If you will tell us your trouble—for obviously some personal trouble has brought you here—I may be able to form an opinion as to whether I can help you.'

As he ceased speaking he handed the stranger a box of cigars. Traske selected one, lit it, and glanced at us in turn as if he were anxious to read our faces.

'First of all,' he said, 'I had better begin at the beginning, and tell you something of myself and of my circumstances. I am the present head of the Traske family, which has held the manor of Penbillo since the fourteenth century. I am a bachelor, and when I die everything on the entail will pass to a young nephew of mine in New Zealand. The immediate past has not been a happy time for land-owners; but I have always lived quietly, and without being wealthy I am entirely free of financial anxieties. It would not be too much to say that for a long while I scarcely knew the meaning of trouble, until my dear sister died about a year ago. What this loss meant to me I despair of being able to make you realise.

'My sister Julia was a spinster some fifteen months younger than me. We had similar tastes and sympathies; we lived together, she keeping house for me; and the closeness of our ages had made us lifelong companions. We elderly folk cling to those whose memories travel back along the same roads as our own, and when Julia was taken from me there was nobody left with whom I could talk intimately of our dear parents or discuss memories of events dating back to childhood. I had never sought friends, and it was with a shock that I came suddenly to realise that I had none. I went through a period of utter loneliness and depression, an experience so desolating that I can hardly bring myself to recall it. It was at that time, Mr Chard, that I began to speculate seriously on the possibility of communicating with those who are no longer with us.'

Chard inclined his head and smiled comprehendingly.

'It is generally a great loss, such as yours, which induces people to take the first step, Mr Traske.'

'Well, I began to read a great deal on the subject, and most of what I read entirely failed to satisfy me. Almost I dismissed it all impatiently as being an outrage on the intelligence of any sane man. Besides, I did not wish merely to receive messages from Julia. I did not wish to hear inanities, purporting to come from her, from the lips of some hired exploiter of sacred things. I wanted to see her sometimes, to be aware of her presence about the house, to feel once more the warmth of that sisterly affection which never failed me while she lived. With these ends in view I did something, Mr Chard, which may very likely provoke your derision.

'You may be well aware that Cornwall is unlike the rest of England; indeed, it is not England at all. We speak of "going to England" when we intend crossing the Tamar. To us an Englishman is a foreigner, and in us you will not find the same mixture of races. I could take you to places where there is not one drop of Saxon blood among the whole of the inhabitants. We are a secretive, conservative, clannish people, who have somehow escaped going with the great tide which is rightly or wrongly called progress. Things are believed in and practised which would be inconceivable to the average person of today. Witchcraft, ill-wishing, black and white magic! Would it surprise you to know, Mr Chard, that just outside the Duchy—in Devonport, to be more precise—there is a white witch with a regular practice who does a roaring trade?'

'It doesn't surprise me at all,' said Chard. 'I happen to know the lady.'

'Ah, then you know something of Cornish witchcraft?'

'Something. I know that such things as blood-stopping, infesting with vermin, charming and cursing are still attempted. There are still women who put needles and pins in a bowl of water. I also know that certain astonishing results have sometimes been obtained.'

Traske leaned forward, looking closely at Chard.

'You know all that?' he said 'Then how do you account for—for certain unquestionable results?'

'Ninety-five per cent of those results are obtained in a manner which I can easily account for. In other words, ninety-five per cent of what passes for witchcraft is sheer humbug. I will go into that matter with you some time if you are interested.'

'But the other five per cent.'

'The other five per cent,' Chard confessed, 'I don't account for at all.'

Traske uttered a sigh and nervously broke the ash from his cigar.

'Mr Chard,' he said, 'in my loneliness and depression, and in my extreme need to see and speak once more to my dear sister, I consulted a certain woman in the village. She told me to return home and gave me certain instructions. I carried them out. '

'Among them,' said Chard drily, 'you had to see that every door and window in the house was open.'

Traske started violently.

'Mr Chard,' he said, 'I swore an oath to that woman that I would keep entirely secret the things she told me to do.'

'I know most of the ritual. Among other things, you had to say, "Woman, come back to me." But don't be alarmed, Mr Traske. I shall not ask you to break your oath. Well, you returned home and did as you were bid. And what happened?'

'That is what has brought me here. And now that I am here I have so little to tell. I have no great gift for description. I doubt if I can make you understand how I have been driven almost to my last extremity. Put into words, it must all sound so slight and vague and unworthy of attention. If I were to hear the same story from another man I should merely say that he was a neurotic, and advise him to see a doctor.'

'Never mind, Mr Traske. Perhaps you will find us a little more sympathetic.'

'On the night when I conducted the experiment nothing seemed to happen at all. I went and sat in my library, hoping and half expecting to see Julia at any moment. I listened for her voice, for the whisper of her gown across the floor, but I heard nothing. I put out my hand for her to touch, and felt nothing. At last I went to bed, utterly disappointed and having lost all faith. It was not until the following night that I was sensible of—in one respect—not having entirely failed.

'I had just heard the gong and come downstairs to eat my lonely dinner. As I was about to enter the dining-room I felt that someone awaited me inside. I entered and found the room empty so far as my eyes and ears were concerned, but I was still aware of that presence. If I could make you understand how strong that impression was I am sure you would not ascribe it to mere nerves or imagination.

'At first—for a minute or two—I was unconscious of any particular emotion, save one of awe. And then, as the undeveloped sense which had made me aware of it grew keener, I realised that, whatever might be in the room with me, it was not Julia. Julia would never have inspired me with the horror and fear and hatred which I felt creeping over me. Directly I had realised that the Presence was not Julia's, I tried to persuade myself that there was nothing there. But I tried in vain, and my sense of perception only strengthened.

'Let me be as clear as I can. The Presence was not all-pervading. Just as it had characteristics, so it also had place and position. Moving about the room I felt myself approaching it or drawing further away. In a little while I could have touched it, had it been tangible. It was sitting—and although I saw nothing, I use that word advisedly—in a chair about halfway down the long dining-room table. When I took my own place at the head of the table, a ghastly thing happened. I felt it change its place and come and sit next to me, at my very elbow. And I knew that this Tiling was beastly and malevolent. Something had entered the house on the previous night in response to my invitation to Julia—something that was not good, but evil. I had opened my house to Love, and Hate had come instead.

'There was three weeks ago. Not for one moment, waking or sleeping, have I been free in my own house from the tyranny of that presence. Not that it is always in the room with me; I feel it enter and I feel it go. I have not seen or heard anything, I have not felt anything in the fleshy sense; but I have been poignantly aware of it in some way which I can neither account for nor describe.

'I realise that this must sound to you like the ravings of a disordered mind. Still, I feel that I must tell you everything. This Thing which has taken possession of my house is possessed of the cruellest and bitterest hatred for me. In me it has inspired a deeper hatred than ever I could have believed a man of my normally mild passions to be capable of feeling. I can truthfully say that I hate it even more than I fear it.

'It would attack me if it could. It would tear me to pieces. I have felt that. I have felt it try. I have felt it rush at me like a silent tempest. I have surmised that my flesh is a barrier between us, and part of my dread is lest this barrier may not be altogether intangible or impassable. It seems to be entirely devoid of reason, for I have done nothing to deserve this hellish spite of anyone, living or dead I entreat you to believe me, Mr Chard. I beg you to believe that my peace of mind is being robbed, and my health undermined, by an invisible and silent, presence which hates me and would do me a mischief if it could.'

He came to a pause. Chard looking fixedly out of the window, asked him a question almost with an air of abstraction:

'Do you know what this presence is like in appearance?'

'Yes.'

Chard stared at him.

'I thought you had seen nothing?' he said.

'Nor have I. But I have some vague perception of what it would be like if I could see it. I know that it is small. I know that it is feminine, and I know that it is monstrously hideous. I can give you no closer description than that. My mind can get no clearer glimpse of it than if it were something moving swiftly and seen out of the tail of my eye.'

Chard seemed to ponder this, saying nothing for some little while.

During the pause Traske sat fidgeting and anxiously regarding him.

'Are you, so far as you know, the only person in the house aware of this unwelcome presence?' Chard asked at last.

'I can't say for certain. I've thought some of the servants looked fidgety and scared of late.'

'You haven't questioned them?'

'How could I, Mr Chard? There has been nothing to see or hear. They might have thought me mad.'

'Yes, I can understand,' Chard agreed. 'Now, Mr Traske, a little while back I think you said that sleeping and waking you had been feeling the tyranny of that presence. Did you mean that it affected you while you were asleep?'

'Well, I've been having bad dreams. But they may have been caused entirely by the nervous state induced by what I had been through.'

'Bad dreams about anything in particular?'

'I don't remember anything of them very clearly, but they were not healthy dreams.'

'You can't remember anything about them at all, then?' Chard urged. Traske uttered a little nervous laugh, the laugh of a man who feels a little foolish at the prospect of causing derision.

'Yes,' he said, 'I seem to have been dreaming a lot about monkeys. As I have said, I can't remember any of the details of my dreams, but I always wake with a vague memory of having been visited by hideous monkey faces in my sleep. '

If Chard felt any inclination to smile he did not show it.

'You will forgive this catechism,' he said. 'It is only by asking questions that I can arrive at any theory. I should like to know if your house was ever supposed to be haunted?'

'Oh, yes,' said Traske, and smiled nervously again. 'A house of that size and age—parts of it are pre-Elizabethan—is certain to have a legendary ghost or two, especially a house situated in that part of the country. I should think local superstition credits us with at least a dozen.

But I never saw one, nor did my parents before me, nor have I ever heard of one being seen.'

'Only one more question, then, Mr Traske,' Chard said smiling. 'Have you any old family records which might mention any such hauntings in the past?'

'I have a diary in manuscript kept by an ancestor of mine in the seventeenth century. He must have been a contemporary of Pepys, for he mentions being in London at the time of the Blessed Restoration, as he was pleased to call it. I cannot, however, pretend to have read it throughout. It has curiously little of historical or family interest,'—here Traske paused and coughed primly—'and he was unpleasantly frank about his love-affairs, which were many and variegated. '

'I see!' Chard said and laughed. 'Well, at the peril of being scandalised, it may be necessary for somebody to look closely into that diary. One should never leave unexplored any possible source of information. You have told us a deeply interesting story, Mr Traske.'

Traske smiled ruefully.

'A little too interesting from my point of view,' he remarked. 'Is it too early to ask if you can make head or tail of it?'

Chard regarded the blue sky through the upper panes of the window.

'I won't ask your forgiveness,' he said, 'for being sceptical. I warned you I always was.'

The visitor's face fell.

'Am I to understand, then,' he asked, almost pitifully, 'that you think I am being deluded by my own imagination? I had despaired from the beginning of making you realise'

'Don't distress yourself on that score,' Chard interrupted quickly and kindly. 'You could hardly have made a plainer or more concise statement. I must be permitted to consider the possibility of your having deluded yourself. But there is equally the possibility that you have not.'

Traske fidgeted and leaned forward in his chair.

'And in that latter event?' he asked. 'In heaven's name, Mr Chard, what manner of thing is plaguing me?'

He was spilling ash over his clothes and Chard got up to find him an ash-tray.

'It is rather early yet to begin theorising,' he said when he had resumed his seat. 'You have, of course, conducted a rather dangerous experiment. Not only the Mosaic Law, but most of the modem churches warn their adherents against attempting to raise spirits or to communicate with those who have passed on to another plane. When you made the effort to bring your sister back you left your house open in something more than the literal sense.

Suppose, in the literal sense, you left your house open and unguarded in the hope that a friend might enter, what would be likely to happen? You would be taking at least equal chances that the first to enter might not be a friend.

Some thief or some enemy who had long been waiting his chance might seize the opportunity. When people learn to cease meddling with things they do not understand—and are not intended to understand—there will be a great deal less trouble in this world, and a great deal less madness.'

Traske listened to this homily without the least sign of resentment.

Indeed, he seemed to brighten under this gentle lashing.

'Am I to take it from that,' he asked eagerly, 'that you—that you think it worthwhile to investigate my trouble?'

'Tomorrow,' said Chard, with a glance at me, 'we shall both be at your service.'

I thought it strange at the time that Traske had not re-enlisted the help of the woman in the village whom he held responsible for what had happened. That point came up later, at one of our many subsequent discussions; for Traske remained in town until we were ready to leave. It seemed that he had been to see her again, and that she had mumbled and looked wise, but was obviously quite ignorant of the nature of the trouble or of the means of overcoming it.

On the following morning we took the long journey to Cornwall, all three of us together, travelling by the Cornish Riviera express, and afterwards by a slow local train from a junction, which set us down at Penbillo early in the evening.

Penbillo we found to be a small fishing village built like a bird's nest in a hollow of enormous cliffs. The Ford car which met us at the station struggled up a mountainous hill a mile and a half long, and dived and climbed alternately for another mile and a half; for the Manor House of Penbillo is three good miles from the village.

The house was completely hidden from any of the roads by a dense screen of trees. Apart from its four lodges no human habitation seemed near, although there must have been farms hidden away in the folds of the hills.

As Traske had led us to expect, the house was very old, but for me it lacked the charm of many old houses. It was gloomy and bare and cold, and the comfort-loving strain of Philistinism in me went crying for certain amenities which have come to be regarded as necessities by this generation.

There were plenty of evidences of wealth. Some of the furniture was almost priceless. An occasional threadbare carpet or torn curtain was merely an indication that Traske could not be troubled to remedy such minor defects. Not to particularise: the house seemed to need that feminine touch of genius which makes a home. Perhaps things had been otherwise in Miss Traske's day. Certainly Traske kept a housekeeper, but she existed solely to supervise the female staff and have charge of the linen and household accounts. Although he took some trouble to ensure our comfort it was easy to see that Traske had already fallen into the careless and untidy ways of most bachelors who live alone.

If ever a house looked haunted it was Penbillo Manor, although, in spite of its traditional ghosts, there had been no disturbances for many years prior to Traske's experiment. One passed through the main entrance into a great baronial hall, in which only one oil lamp burned high in the ceiling, and gave no more light than one of those lamps which are kept burning in sanctuaries. The dining-room was a fine room with panelled walls and two great carved fireplaces facing each other across its width, and as severe and scantily furnished as a monastic refectory. Besides a great sideboard there was only a long table which hid the seats of a double row of massive oak chairs. Here lamps were not used, but five-stemmed silver candelabra stood at intervals along the table. There were lighted candles in these when we came down to dinner.

After entering the house Chard said no word to our host concerning the cause of our visit, but he induced him to produce the diary of Rowland Traske, Esquire, gentleman, of Penbillo Manor in the Duchy of Cornwall—or, rather, that portion of it dated between 1659 and 1664, which had escaped destruction in defiance of the writer's last wishes. It had been bound in great dingy boards, like an old bible, and Chard spent an hour and a half before dinner with that mighty tome. I heard Chard laughing over it once or twice.

'The scandalous old gentlemen who write their reminiscences nowadays,' he said by way of explanation, 'don't know the elements of their business.'

We were waited on at dinner by a lean, sepulchral butler of venerable years, who would have lent a certain eeriness to the dining-room of a brand-new suburban flat, freshly furnished by Drage's. He maintained his post behind his master's chair for the greater part of his time, looking like an allegorical figure of Death at a feast; and while he was in the room we talked little. Still, he had brought Burgundy to exactly the right temperature, and that was something. He had just set a dish before his master, when Traske glanced at him over his shoulder and said, 'Don't forget to remind Annie about hot-water bottles for these gentlemen, Puckey.'

'Mrs Mason has given instructions, I believe, sir,' the old man replied.

'Annie has gone.'

'Gone?'

'Yes, sir. Left. I believe she has found a situation in Looe. She imagined monkeys.'

I saw Traske wince.

'Imagined monkeys?' he repeated. 'What do you mean?'

'I don't know, sir. It was what she said. It happened the first night you were away. She dreamed about monkeys, and it upset her. Mrs Mason tried to reason with her, but she wouldn't stay.'

I could see that Traske wanted to ask more, but it was not the time or place to discuss with his butler the vagaries of the lower servants. At last, when the finger-bowls were on the table and Puckey had removed his funereal presence from the room, Traske turned quickly to Chard and said,

'What do you make of that? That girl Annie. She dreamed of monkeys, just as I've been dreaming of them. And it's frightened her away.'

'It's interesting, certainly,' said Chard in his calm, non-committal manner. What else he might have said was checked by a sudden change in Traske's manner. He grimaced suddenly as if with pain and leaned towards Chard.

'Don't you feel anything?' he whispered.

Chard's chin jerked up an inch and he sat very still. Traske turned to me at his elbow and whispered hoarsely and appealingly, 'Don't you feel it? It's in the room! It's just come in!'

For a long minute we three sat as still as stones. I looked about me as stealthily and guiltily as a thief in hiding, but I could see nothing; I listened, but I could hear nothing. Then Chard rose almost lazily.

'It's in the room, you say?' he asked in his quiet, cheerful, measured voice.

'Yes.' Traske's voice fell hushed and hoarse and awed. 'It's in one of those chairs on your side ... the third or fourth ... I can't quite tell.'

Chard went and stood behind the two chairs.

He slapped his hands down firmly on their backs.

'One of these?' he asked.

'Yes . . . Can't you feel anything?'

Chard laughed.

'That,' he said, 'is hardly a fair question. You have introduced more than a little suggestion. Do you think you feel anything, Torrance?'

I could only say that I felt exceedingly uncomfortable, which was true enough. But whatever my sensations, they could have been in no degree as keen as Traske's. I saw horror, fear and hatred spread over his weak and rather foolish old face. He rose, shaking.

'If you gentlemen don't mind,' he stammered, 'we will smoke our cigars in the library.'

To my surprise Chard agreed cheerfully enough. I had expected him to wait a little and demand to experimentalise.

'By all means,' he said; and within half a minute we were following Traske across the hall. But he had barely reached the door when he turned to announce hopelessly that It was following us.

I shall never forget that evening. Traske was hounded from room to room by that unseen malevolent presence, and we with him. There might have been an element of farce in the situation, but I for one was only too keenly aware of the horrible and the grotesque. Traske would go to cross the room and stop and turn away, like a man baulked by traffic in the act of crossing a street. Possibly his sensations were infectious, for I was soon in a mood to imagine almost anything. We endured this sort of thing for an hour or so, and then went to bed.

'Well,' said Chard to me on our way up, 'feel anything?'

'I don't know,' I replied.

'A highly scientific answer,' he returned gravely. 'I don't know either. I suppose you didn't happen to catch yourself thinking about monkeys?'

A shiver ran through me.

'I hate the beasts!' I said.

'H'm! They're not nice animals. But you've never had anything to do with them. Ever catch yourself hating them before?'

I had to reflect.

'No,' I admitted; and then added, 'That's funny.'

'Not funny,' said Chard, 'but interesting. Well, good night.'

Chard spent nearly all the following day with the diary, and Traske, who seemed glad to get out of the house on any pretext, tramped about the estate with me, showing me objects of no particular interest to anybody but himself. On our return in the evening, after a long walk in the afternoon, I could tell by a quiet gleam of triumph in Chard's eye that he was on the trail of something. Presently he found an opportunity of taking me on one side.

'You'd better not take port after dinner,' he said. 'Help yourself to a good stiff brandy. You may need it.'

He begged a question, but declined to answer it when it was put.

'I don't promise anything,' he said, 'but something may happen. And if anything does, for God's sake keep your head and keep quiet. I warn you that if we see anything it will not be nice to look at.'

In vain I tried to question him further. He would say nothing. So at eight o'clock we sat down for the second time at that gloomy dinner-table we were waited on as before by the sepulchral Puckey, and in most details everything was as it had been on the preceding evening. As before, Puckey left us when dessert, finger-bowls, port and brandy were set out before us. The door had hardly closed behind him when Chard glanced under the table.

'Mr Traske has dropped his table-napkin,' he remarked. 'It's on your side, Torrance.'

Courtesy compelled me to stoop and grope. Courtesy also compelled Traske to stoop and grope. Between us we retrieved it. Then, bearing in mind Chard's advice, I helped myself to brandy. I was sipping it when, a few moments later, I was startled to hear a loud yawn from Traske. He looked up at me, a foolish smile of apology on his face.

'Ton my word ... I'm so sorry ... I've come over sleepy ... I don't understand.'

'Never mind,' said Chard. 'You've done a lot of walking.'

'But I feel strange ... my head ...'

He made as if to rise, but Chard quietly pushed him back into his chair.

'Don't let us disturb you,' he said. 'Sleep there, if you wish. It will do you good. '

Traske seemed to struggle for a moment. Then he gave it up and, breathing strenuously, fell forward across the table.

I stared at Chard in alarm and dismay, but he smiled back reassuringly.

'He won't hurt,' he remarked. 'He'll sleep like a top for hours. I doped his wine while you and he were groping for his table napkin.'

And he took from his pocket a little white packet, and showed it to me.

'But why on earth'

'Because it was the most convenient way of being with him while he was asleep. The presence which haunts him is also battening on him. While he is asleep he is even more fully aware of it. He dreams of monkey faces.

Also, while he is asleep it may derive power from him to materialise. And I think, while we are about it, we might have this in readiness.'

'This,' was a small bottle which he took from his breast pocket and set down upon the table. His fingers began to busy themselves with the stopper

'What's that?' I demanded.

'This,' said Chard, 'is Holy Water. Before piety went out of fashion our ancestors used it with some effect in circumstances such as these. And I warn you that we may be about to raise something which we may not desire to keep in our company too long.'

Even while he spoke I was watching Traske, who was breathing deeply and regularly. But suddenly there came a catch in his breathing, and I saw a tremor pass through him as if his flesh were shrinking from something and were trying to part from his very bones in an ecstasy of revulsion. And at the same time I heard Chard draw a sharp breath, as if at a sudden cold douche, and stumble to his feet.

I turned my gaze upon him. He was looking past me into the middle of the room. His eyes had started to stare, and I knew by the rigidity of his jaws that his teeth were locked. I turned my head and followed the direction of his gaze.

It is not my wish to pile horror upon horror, so I shall describe but briefly what I saw.

Standing between the table and the fireplace behind me was the diminutive figure of a girl or woman. It wore feminine attire, and the fashion of the clothes as not of today, but of some century long past. Girl or woman, it was scarcely four feet high, and monstrously broad and ill-shaped. But the crowning horror of this creature was its face.

It would be wrong to say that it had the face of an ape. The horror was that one could tell at a glance that it was human. But I never saw features so simian on any human countenance.

Its eyes, full of a baleful and malevolent hatred, burned on all of us in turn before transferring the full malignancy of their glare upon the bowed figure of Traske. The room heaved about me as if I were on a ship at sea, and I heard my own voice in a strange, throaty cry.

How long we stood staring at it I cannot say. It seemed minutes to me, but Chard afterwards assured me it was only seconds. During that time the visitant remained as still as ourselves, until without any warning, and with the agility of one of the apes it so resembled, it made a spring at Traske. I heard myself cry out again, and mingled with my cry came the splash of water as Chard flung the contents of the bottle. Instantly the Thing stopped.

It lurched and writhed. Its mouth fell open, working its bestial grimaces.

Silently it thrashed about it with its limbs. It was like some foul thing which had taken a mortal wound. The teeth champed and the writhing lips framed—it seemed to me—words too foul for any human language.

I felt my senses going. When they returned Chard was bending over me forcing brandy between my lips.

'It's gone now, old chap,' he said quietly. 'Feel better? Sorry' I let you in for that. '

Shaking all over I let him help me up.

'You'll see no more of that tonight,' he murmured reassuringly.

'What devil was it?' I managed to ask.

'I'll explain it all to you presently after we've carried our host to bed. Let me know' when you feel strong enough to help me lift him. We don't want the servants to know. This is what people who try to raise spirits are liable to get!'

Two hours later I sat in Chard's bedroom, and he held the great diary between his knees.

'I was right,' he said, 'in looking here for a clue. I think this entry will explain everything. It is dated the eighteenth of December, 1663. Mr Rowland Traske was here at the time. Listen!

' "Was importuned for a dole his morning by old Mistress Russet, her man being kept from work by a quinsy. Did give her what she asked, she having been nurse to us when we were children, and did listen of her to long accounts of old days, she having the clack of a score of fowls. One of her tales did mightily tickle my ribs. On her authority, in the day of my great-grandsire, there was born to him and his lady a hideous female child, so like an ape that they durst let nobody see it for very shame. This Monster they hid away in a closet, spreading abroad the conceit that it had died presently after birth, none tending it save themselves and one trusted servant. As the Creature grew, so did its humours come to match the foulness of its face and form, until the Squire did verily believe that 'twas some by-blow of Satan. When it died after many years 'twas said he smothered it. But if that be true or false, the horrid shape of this Monster continued to haunt the house, showing all the naughtiness and hatred of a fiend from the pit, till a Jesuit from Exeter did presently come and exorcise it. I did tell Mistress Russet that if my lady durst present me with such a Devil's bantling I would smother it at birth and hazard finding a Jesuit to exorcise it later, Jesuits being scarce in these days. Whereat she laughed and thought I jested, though I spoke soberly.'"

Chard ceased reading and laid aside the book.

'And now,' he said, 'you know as much as I know. You can picture that wretched, imprisoned girl, whose spirit grew as hideous as her face and form, burning with hatred against the family who hid her away and treated her like a wild beast, and who later, probably, murdered her. That spirit haunted the house in all its ugliness and naked hatred as we saw it tonight, until, as you have just heard, it was exorcised. It could not return then, until somebody invited it back. Traske did not know he was inviting it, but, as I have explained to him, he left his house open, and this enemy, who had long been awaiting the opportunity, came in. Such cases are not nearly so uncommon as many people would suppose.'

There was a long pause.

'And what will you do now?' I asked.

'Oh, I shall advise Traske to go away for a time.'

'But will that'

'No. While he is away he will have to arrange for certain things to be done. Exorcism was successful in the previous instance, and should be so again. Many people do not know that the power of exorcism is given to one priest in every diocese, and that the power is still used. At least I do not know of any other remedy, and our friend Traske must please himself.'

The Third Visitation

It is obviously my task to select for publication only such of the adventures of Francis Chard as may be termed successful and have at the same time a dramatic value. Of course, he, and I with him, had hundreds of disappointments. Often the ghost refused flatly to show itself while we were in the house, and sometimes we were able to deduce that it existed only in the imagination of the person who had enlisted Chard's aid. Real ghosts were few and far between, and the experiences recorded are the gleanings of many years of psychic investigation. The very nature of the work, which was at once Chard's hobby and his profession, made him the prey of every kind of lunatic. It would be no new experience to either of us now to be summoned many miles in order to listen to the creaking of a chimney cowl, or suffer at the hands of some fool who thought himself a practical humorist.

But there were cases which promised excitement and intense interest from the very beginning, and such a one was presented by Sir Manning Selchester.

I was not present at the first interview between him and Chard, and I must tell of it as Chard afterwards described it to me. But at least I can describe Sir Manning at first hand, for I was to meet him very shortly afterwards. He was a tall, lean man in the middle fifties, with rather watery blue eyes and fair hair already half turned white, and he wore an old-fashioned frock coat which bore obvious signs of age, baggy trousers, and wrinkled and shabby boots. But he wore his dingy clothes with an assured air of being able to afford to dress as he liked. He was plainly nervous and excited, and, during his interview with Chard he fondled and fidgeted with a dilapidated and shapeless umbrella. He began the interview abruptly.

'Mr Chard,' he said, tremulously, 'I have called to see if you can help me—if you can save me from the dreadful necessity of taking my own life.' Chard regarded him coolly and steadily.

'Whatever your trouble is, you must not do that,' he said. 'I am quite convinced that nobody gains anything by that. The same pains and the same anxieties await them on the other side, perhaps in some terribly magnified forms. But sit down, my dear sir, and let me hear about your troubles. '

Sir Manning sat down.

'I know,' he said, 'that I need not apologise for the story I am about to tell you, for, of course, I am already aware that you believe in these things. You know my name, and perhaps the name of my family is not altogether strange to you.'

Chard inclined his head 'The Selchesters,' he said, 'have helped to make history. The family seat used to be Selchester Court in Wiltshire'

'It is now. I came up from there this morning. Perhaps you have heard, Mr Chard, of a grim story connected with my family.'

'I have it here,' Chard answered, nodding towards one of his shelves. 'It is in a book, Family Legends and Curses, published some twenty years ago. But I should like to hear the story from your own lips, if it is pertinent to the occasion which has brought you here to see me.'

'It is!' said Sir Manning vehemently. 'It is! I think I had best begin by presenting to you what are actually historical facts. In the dining-room at Selchester there is a portrait of Barbara Selchester, an ancestress of mine, painted in the days of Charles the First. The lady is shown wearing a gown of very vivid blue. The picture is excellent as a work of art, but of little intrinsic value. It is unsigned, and is probably the work of a pupil of Van Dyck. It remains, however, one of our most treasured possessions because of the grim story connected with it.

'This Barbara Selchester, who married an ancestor of mine, was one of the Friargate family, and a distant cousin of the ill-fated John Hampden. When the Civil War broke out she was doubtless at heart a Roundhead, although there is no reason to believe that she was otherwise than loyal to her husband, who took up arms for the King.

'In 1643, shortly before the first battle of Newbury, there was a skirmish not far from Selchester, in which a detachment of Parliament troops were routed and pursued. Finding himself close to home, John Selchester went thither for the night, and went straightway to his wife's room. While he was actually on the threshold he heard the snap of a door closing within.

'Now there was a hiding-hole in Mistress Selchester's room, the family having until recently been Papists. John Selchester rushed in, wild with jealousy. I think I had better sacrifice the drama by telling you the facts of the case as briefly as possible. Barbara Selchester had given sanctuary to her own brother, a cornet of horse in the Roundhead army, who had been compelled to fly for his life from the fight in which her husband had been recently engaged.

'John Selchester, misunderstanding his wife's agonised appeals for the attempt of a faithless woman to save her lover, drew his sword, flung open the secret door beside the bed, and stabbed to the heart the shrinking young man who cowered inside. Then, deaf to the explanations of his wife, and misunderstanding the cause of her wild grief, he killed her while she knelt to him imploring his mercy.

'Out of that tragic story there grew another, which most members of my family of recent years have treated as an idle and picturesque legend. The house was supposed to be haunted by Barbara Selchester, but she was seen only occasionally. Her apparition, seen three times within a short period, was supposed to foretell the death, in some terrible form, of the head of the house.

'Now sceptics may think and say what they like, but she was seen three times just before my grandfather was burned to death in his own stables. She was seen three times just before my great-grandfather met his death in a form so horrible that it was kept from me by my parents, and the secret is now mercifully lost. There have been in all half-a-dozen instances covering a period of nearly three hundred years. I don't mind admitting, Mr Chard, that I have always been terrified of Barbara Selchester, and always said that if she made three appearances while I was head of the family I would forestall her by taking my life in some painless manner, for God knows what hideous end might otherwise be in store for me. And now' you have guessed why I have come to you. Mr Chard, she has been seen twice within the last week. '

Chard raised his brows a quarter of an inch. 'Have you seen her?' he asked quietly.

'No.'

'Then who has?'

'Two people in whom I place the most implicit confidence—my niece Marjorie, and Thane, my old butler, who has been in the family service since he was a boy. '

'And where was she seen?'

'In the dining-room, where her portrait hangs.'

'And she was dressed exactly as in the portrait?'

'Yes. But apart from that there could be no mistake. They both agree that the likeness was exact.'

'If you please, I should like a few details.'

'My niece was the first to see her, four nights ago. Just before going to bed she had come into the dining-room for a book which my nephew had last seen there. She had opened the door, but had not crossed the threshold when she saw the figure of a woman standing facing her, with its back to the opposite wall. She recognised it at once, and fled screaming.

'Last night Thane saw it. It is his duty to go round after everybody else is in bed and lock up all the rooms on the ground floor. There are two doors to the dining-room, and he had already locked one and pocketed the key—a door leading to a passage connected with the servants' quarters. Having locked that door he went by the same passage into the hall, locked up other rooms, and at last came to the other door of the dining-room. He looked in to see that everything was in order, and saw the same figure standing in exactly the same spot where my niece had seen it. '

'And what did he do?'

'He too fled. But he had the presence of mind to lock the door behind him, perhaps as a precaution against pursuit. He then shouted for help. I was asleep, but my nephew Philip heard him and rushed downstairs. Together they entered the dining-room and found nothing.'

Chard nodded. 'I understand,' he said, 'that both doors were locked and that thus if anybody had—shall we say?—been playing a practical joke, they must have been found when your nephew and the butler entered.'

'That is quite correct, Mr Chard. They made a most thorough search.' Chard pursed his lips.

'I think I grasp the situation. And now, Sir Manning, I want to ask you two or three questions which you may consider irrelevant. Do you mind telling me how long you have been head of the family?'

'Only five years. I inherited from my elder brother, who never married.'

'And you have an heir of your own?'

'No. I am a widower, and my only son was killed in the war. When I die, the title and estates will pass to my nephew Philip.'

'Ah, the same who came downstairs last night and searched the dining-room with the butler?'

'Exactly, Philip and his sister Marjorie both live with me. He acts as my secretary and agent. He is not unsympathetic, but he does not believe in the curse, or in the supernatural at all. He laughs at his sister, and has since been trying to persuade Thane that he only dreamed he saw something. But it is at his suggestion that I have come to see you. He thinks you may be able to set my mind at rest. '

'I'll do my best, Sir Manning. You mustn't lose heart. When may I come down?'

'Whenever you will. As soon as you may find it convenient. This evening, if you possibly can.'

'I think I can manage that,' Chard said thoughtfully. 'May I bring a friend, a Mr Torrance?'

Sir Manning heaved a sigh of relief.

'My dear Mr Chard,' he said, 'bring anybody whom you are likely to find in the least helpful.'

And now I come into the story.

In the early evening Chard and I caught a fast train to Swindon, and completed the journey by travelling to the fourth or fifth station on a branch line. It took us less than two hours from Paddington, and it could have been scarcely half-past seven when we arrived.

A large car awaited our arrival outside the station, and with it a young man who introduced himself as Philip Selchester. A chauffeur was at the wheel, and young Selchester rode with us inside throughout a five-mile drive.

'Of course' he said, 'you spiritualists and I are at the opposite poles. Frankly, I don't believe in all this. I don't wish to appear snide, but I must at least be honest. The greatest kindness you can do is to convince my uncle that the legend is a pure myth, and that the apparition existed only in the imagination of my sister and of Thane. If somebody else imagines he sees it, the consequences, so far as my uncle is concerned, may be tragic. I fully and seriously believe that he will take his own life.'

Chard did not wince when Philip Selchester called him a spiritualist, although spiritualist he never was.

'I see,' he said, 'you are one of those people whom nothing will convince.'

'Short of seeing the lady for myself; but she has not been so accommodating. And if I saw her I should probably regard her as a hallucination. My uncle enlisted your aid on my advice. I have heard something about you, Mr Chard, and know of—forgive me for saying it so boldly—your reputation for honesty. I could not trust any other spiritualist to be content with finding nothing, and that is what I am sure you will find. I don't believe in the ghost, or in the consequences which are supposed to follow her third visitation: it is my uncle's peace of mind that concerns me.'

Chard turned to him equably.

'I am glad to hear you speak like that,' he said, 'but I am afraid I don't share your optimism. We must face the facts, however unpleasant they may be. In my opinion, the apparition will be seen for the third time, in which case we must not give up hope, but try to find some way of pacifying the offended spirit.'

It occurred to me then that Chard was talking strangely. He had not minded being called a spiritualist, and he had never in his life tried to pacify an offended spirit. Still, it was not my business to talk, and it was as well I realised this.

Selchester Court, from what we could see of its facade in the dark, was a typical Elizabethan country mansion. We entered a fine wide hall strewn with skins, and were greeted by Sir Manning and his niece Marjorie. She was a tall, slender, dark girl, pale but vivacious, and obviously very fond of her uncle. Later in the evening she said to Chard and me, 'I wish I'd realised at the time the effect my experience was bound to have upon my uncle, and said nothing about it. If you see anything don't tell him, don't tell anybody. Promise me.'

'My dear Miss Selchester,' Chard replied kindly, 'you must please remember that I am here to do what I think is best. I have had some experience of these matters, and you must please trust me.'

Dinner had already been put back for our convenience, but Chard seemed quite conscienceless in further disorganising the household timetable. He demanded straightway to be shown over the house, and we visited the dining-room first of all.

This was a fine long room panelled in oak, and furnished almost as severely as a monks' refectory. There were only three pictures, all portraits in oils, and naturally our attention was directed first of all to that of the luckless Barbara Selchester. She was a dark woman with grave eyes, and a great deal of colour in her cheeks, but Chard and I both remarked a certain warm look about her face. Chard, who knew nothing of art, airily attributed this to the influence of the Dutch school.

'It's rather curious,' he said, wrinkling his brows. 'I've certainly never seen the portrait before, and yet the face is vaguely familiar to me. However, it's not worth while speculating on that subject now.'

He then asked Marjorie Selchester to stand exactly in the place where she had seen the apparition, and she placed herself with her back to the wall between the portrait and the fireplace, perhaps a yard and a half distant from either of them. He then asked Thane, the butler, to be sent for, and made of him the same request. Thane stood in precisely the same place.

After which, Chard, from some motive which was not clear to any of us, demanded to see every room in the house, and it must have been after nine o'clock when at last we sat down to a spoilt dinner. This was not served in the dining-room, which had not been used for meals since Miss Selchester's distressing experience. We entered a smaller and friendlier room, and began to discuss the object of our visit as soon as the butler and his two satellites had left us alone. Chard addressed himself to Sir Manning.

'I quite understand how anxious you are,' he said, 'lest the apparition should be seen again; but believe me if that is to happen, it cannot possibly be prevented, and in that event it is better that Torrance or I should see it. There are steps yet to be taken, so do not give way to despair. Torrance, you and I must be prepared for a sleepless night.'

'Does that mean that we are to camp out in the dining-room?' I asked. Chard shook his head.

'No,' he said. 'My experience is that if two people wait in a room in the expectation of seeing something, the something they are expecting to see declines to reveal itself. You must remember that on the two occasions when the apparition was seen, it was seen by two people who walked hastily into the room. I think we will stay outside, and pay frequent visits throughout the night. '

'I leave everything to you,' said Sir Manning dully.

'One thing I want to warn you about,' said Chard, turning to me. 'If you see anything, don't for Heaven's sake try to touch it. Remember, we shall be dealing with a highly malignant spirit, and to attempt to interfere with it might be dangerous to life or reason.'

I suppressed a gasp of astonishment. This was not in the least like Chard. I knew him well enough to detect the insincerity of his tone. He was acting fairly well, but not well enough to deceive me.
'Well then, what am I to do?' I asked.

'Do nothing,' he returned. 'Look at it, and then go away. You probably won't want to stop,' he added grimly.

I was uncomfortable all the while until Sir Manning and his nephew and niece retired to bed. There was something going on in Chard's mind of which I had not the least inkling. About an hour after dinner the others left us to our work of investigation, when Chard resumed his chair and dragged it a little nearer to the fire.

'The trap having been efficiently baited,' he said, helping himself to a cigarette, 'I think we may count ourselves very unfortunate if the lady declines to show herself. What's the time? A quarter to twelve. We may as well have one look now, and if there's nothing there, we can make ourselves comfortable for a few minutes.

He rose and walked across the hall to the door of the dining-room, I following him. There was no light inside, but enough streamed past us from the hall to give the room a certain faint illumination. There was nothing there, and we closed the door and returned together.

'I should think roughly twelve o'clock will be about the time,' said Chard sitting down again. 'According to most people who are unlearned on the subject, the witching hour of midnight is the time when all properly constituted ghosts choose to revisit the scenes of their earthly life. I feel sure that this one will be so obliging as not to keep us up too late.'

This again was very unlike Chard.

'What on earth is the matter with you tonight?' I asked. 'What have you got in your head? Do you think all this is a joke, or what?'

Instantly his face darkened.

'No,' he said, 'it isn't a joke.'

'Then what do you really think?' I demanded.

'That,' he answered, 'I hope to be able to tell you in ten minutes' time.'

I knew it was no use trying to draw him, and we sat on, talking at intervals for the next few minutes, until the stable clock outside struck twelve times. Chard glanced towards the door and got upon his legs.

'Don't be nervous,' he said, 'and don't mind what I do, but for goodness sake, keep your eyes open.'

We crossed the hall once more, and Chard flung open the door of the dining-room. I knew by the instant rigidity of his pose that there was something there, and hastily looking over his shoulder I saw it for myself. With its back to the wall, midway between the fire and the portrait stood the figure of a woman. In almost every detail of dress and feature she was the exact replica of the lady of the portrait, and she stared at us across the room out of seemingly dull and sightless eyes. We stood staring at it for a long moment and then Chard acted with disconcerting swiftness. He bounded across the room and flung himself upon the figure.

Chard was an old rugger player and, instinctively, I suppose, he collared it low around the knees. Instantly I was aware of a struggle going on. A strange, jerky and yet lifeless sort of animation—if I may be permitted a contradiction in terms—seemed to take possession of the woman's figure. I came running around the long table to Chard's assistance, and as I reached him he fell back heavily against me and knocked me spinning. And as I fell I heard a muffled oath and the low click of a latch.

'Matches!' said Chard sharply.

'Have you got her?' I gasped.

'Got part of her,' he answered. 'One of her legs, poor dear! You never met a ghost with a wooden leg before, did you?'

I scrambled up, struck a match, and gazed at that which Chard was nursing in his arms. It was a complete lady's leg, with an old-fashioned buckled shoe upon the foot, and a green silk stocking reaching above the knee. Modesty did not curtail my gaze, for the thigh was quite shapeless, and made of unvarnished wood. The wooden joint which attached it to the body had been splintered in the struggle.

'Well, I'm damned!' I exclaimed.

'If Master Philip has his wish, we both are,' Chard observed. 'The question is, shall we relieve Sir Manning's mind now, or go to bed and say nothing? I imagine our friend Philip will take the hint, and will clear out as soon as possible. If we give him time we may save the old man and the girl an embarrassing scene. Yes, I think we'll go back to the morning-room and have a smoke and a drink.'

'I had an instinct that things were as they have turned out to be during my interview with Sir Manning this morning,' said Chard to me a little later.

'When a man announces his intention of committing suicide painlessly to save himself from some frightful death in the event of the family apparition being seen three times, there is every reason for the apparition to be seen as many times as may be necessary—if someone has anything to gain by his death. Obviously Philip Selchester had. He is, or was, the heir, and his uncle might go on living for another twenty years. There were other details which I found interesting, such as the lady appearing in exactly the same dress as the one in the portrait. Why? The portrait was probably painted some years before her death. People don't have their portraits painted in the middle of the Great Rebellion, and surely the unfortunate woman hadn't to make one dress last her from 1641 to 1643.

'Then again, the hiding-hole in the bedroom interested me, and the fact that the Selchesters had previously been Catholics. People who hid priests in those days had more than one hiding-place. That gave me an idea as to how the "apparition" could appear and disappear even when it was locked inside the room. The fact that after the butler had seen the supposed ghost Mr Philip came downstairs rather baffled me at first. Then I hit upon the right solution, which was confirmed by my examination of the house. There is a big, old-fashioned cupboard in it. If I'm not much mistaken, there's a false floor to that cupboard, and a secret staircase leading down to a chamber behind the panels in the dining-room. I needn't expatiate on the convenience to people in the bad old days of a secret hiding-place with entrances and exits on two different floors.

'Now, Philip Selchester probably found the secret hiding-place by accident, and said nothing about it, with the intention of turning it to some account, and here he was helped by a piece of sheer chance.

'You know I said that I had seen someone very like the lady in the portrait. About a year ago I walked into a waxwork exhibition at a country fair, and saw for the first time the waxwork face which we both saw tonight. It was supposed to represent Anne Boleyn, or somebody like that, and although it isn't exactly like the face of the portrait, it is near enough to pass muster. I should like to wager that Philip Selchester saw the same waxwork, that it put ideas into his head, and that he bought it. It was comparatively simple to get a dress made exactly like the one in the picture. And when he had smuggled the dummy figure into the house he could keep it quite safely in the secret closet.

'The rest is quite simple. Having lifted the dummy figure out into the room he needed only to keep open the hidden door in the panels wide enough for his hand to come through to support it, and the body of the figure propped against the wall hid him securely. When I pounced on it tonight we had a tug of war. I suppose he can claim to have won since he got most of the lady, but I am quite satisfied to have got away with a leg. I was rather afraid that he wouldn't produce his ghost for our benefit, until I managed to allay his fears by telling you in his presence on no account to touch it. That was just what the young man wanted. He must have been delighted at the prospect of showing his ghost to somebody who could be guaranteed not to interfere with it.'

I looked at Chard, and began to laugh helplessly, but presently I grew grave again and said, 'Do you really think he did it in the hope that his uncle would commit suicide?'

'Never a doubt,' Chard replied. 'At least, I should say that Sir Manning has plenty of evidence if he wants to get the entail broken. Whether he will use it or not I can't say. And now what about turning in? I'm going to take that leg with me and sleep with it under the bolster. It's very important!'

We were up early next morning, but not so early as Philip Selchester. We learned that he had left hurriedly in his own two-seater. Later on, when Sir Manning had nearly finished trying to thank us, we spent a pleasant morning prospecting for the secret hiding-place. We found our way to it at last through the cupboard in Philip's room. At the bottom of a very narrow flight of stairs, lying in a dusty chamber behind the dining-room wall, we found the dummy figure of a lady with hands and face made out of wax, clad in a blue dress of a fashion three centuries old. The unfortunate 'lady' had a leg missing.

The Woman with Three Eyes

Chard and I were lucky in getting a good train to Surbiton. Most of those green electric trains stop at every station, but there are a few fast ones put on in the early evening for the spatted and umbrella'd City men who can afford to live in the Thames Valley, and we were lucky enough to catch one. Ours, while it showed a proper diffidence in negotiating the labyrinths between Waterloo and Clapham Junction, made only one official stop, at Wimbledon.

The journey occupied about twenty minutes, which Chard and I spent in talking.

'I should really like to know what you think of all this,' said Chard, leaning over to me. 'A suburban house which is suddenly haunted by two people, one of them a woman with three eyes, is surely a novelty.'

'I shan't believe in her,' I said, 'until I see her.'

'Two servants and Mr and Mrs Grantley Scottman have both seen her.'

'But only the servants have seen the three eyes. One imagined that extraordinary detail and told the other, who also imagined it in sympathy.'

'Well, it's queer enough without that. Here's a modem suburban house which the Scottmans bought three years ago. They've lived in it comfortably until the last fortnight, when all manner of disturbances break out. They hear explosions like revolver shots, always two at a time, and they meet unexpectedly and in different rooms a stout pale-haired woman who, according to some witnesses has three eyes, and a tall fleshy-faced man with a red moustache, who sometimes has a glass in his hand and is seen hovering about by the telephone. Both these people are apparently as substantial as we are, and they both wear modem dress, but they have no business to be in the house and they have an extraordinary knack of disappearing.'

'If it's a true psychic manifestation,' I suggested, 'the modem clothes narrow the field of investigation down to recent times, and the post-war history of the house should be readily obtainable.'

'Well, it is and it isn't. Scottman bought the house off an outside broker named Gallop, who now lives at Wimbledon. Both Gallop and his wife apparently live the blameless and brainless lives of well-to-do Suburbia. But if anything very unusual happened in the house while they were there, the Scottmans might easily know nothing about it. It isn't like living in the country. Tragedies in a place like Surbiton are soon forgotten. One doesn't know one's next door neighbour, and if one does he is probably a new-comer to the neighbourhood. The servants are not local products. They are imported from the country and from the working-class areas of London, and when they leave a situation the chances are greatly against their taking another in the same district. Surbiton is one of those places without traditions or memories The stock-jobbers have driven away the retired colonels and old maids who used to live there. It's a camping-ground for them on their way up to Park Lane, or on their way back to oblivion. But of course in the present case one can always make inquiries of these Gallops.'

We found Mr Grantley Scottman and a car awaiting us at Surbiton station. Scottman had called on Chard, but I now met him for the first time. He was a youngish man with a good appearance, pleasant manners and a cultured voice, and he was not in the least typical of the neighbourhood in which he lived. I was soon to learn that he hated Surbiton with a deep and bitter hatred, and that he had bought a house there in deference to his wife's wishes. It seemed that she wanted to be near town and that she was fond of the river.

The car, a limousine driven by a liveried chauffeur, bore us swiftly and silently over the tram-route towards Kingston, and turned suddenly into a wide, gravelled road, lined with pretentious houses, each standing aloof in its own two or three acres of sedate gardens. Scottman's house was hidden behind a shrubbery. There were two gates connected by an arc of drive, to which the house stood at a tangent. It was a red-brick, late Victorian monstrosity, designed and built by men who had sold their souls to the devil of ugliness.

Scottman let us into the house where we were encountered by a youngish butler, who had obviously been a soldier. He relieved us of our hats, coats and suit-cases, and our host threw open a door at the end of the hall. 'Come into my study, won't you?' he said. 'There's time for a drink and a chat before you go up to dress. My wife's out, but she'll be in at any moment now. '

It was a pleasant room, decorated with curios and hunting trophies. Scottman asked us to sit down and produced a tantalus and a syphon.

'Anything fresh?' Chard asked him.

'Nothing since I saw you this morning. There hasn't been time. It's hardly dark yet. '

'I mean, is there anything you forgot to tell me? I'd like you to go over the ground in case there is, and for the benefit of my friend here. '

Scottman looked at me and uttered a laugh which sounded hollow and abashed.

'This is a crazy business, Mr Torrance,' he said. 'At least, it seems so to me. But perhaps you have always believed in such things, or have had previous experiences. I don't mind owning that I'd never believed such things could happen, and I'd classed all who didn't agree with me as so many cranks. Even when I went to see Mr Chard this morning I expected to interview somebody with a white face, long hair and wild eyes. I was agreeably surprised.

'Well, now, I was the first to see one of them—I don't know what you'd call them—ghosts, I suppose. I'd been up to town, and couldn't get back until after the usual dinner-time, so I'd phoned to have the meal put back half an hour.

'When I got in my wife was already dressing, and I walked in here to leave some papers before going upstairs. There was no light in the room, but plenty streamed past me from the hall, and I could see quite clearly. There was a man standing over there by the telephone, with the receiver to his ear. He was a big man with a reddish moustache and stiff, upstanding grey hair, and one of those bloated, purplish faces. Although he was one of the most vulgar-looking beasts I've ever seen I couldn't help supposing that he was some acquaintance of my wife's whom she'd brought in with her, and who'd asked to use the phone. He'd no air at all of having no business in my study, and seemed not in the least surprised to see me, so I didn't question him and took him for granted. I only hoped that the brute wasn't staying to dinner.

'You can't talk much to people when they're using the phone, so I just said, "Oh, hadn't you better have some light?" And with that I turned on the electric switch and closed the door on him.

'A few moments later, as I was passing through my wife's room to get to mine, I said, "Hallo, my dear, who's the bad bit of work I found in my study?" She didn't seem to tumble, and when I explained matters she told me she didn't know of any such person. That was quite enough for me, so I hared downstairs to kick him out, and found nobody. I questioned the servants, and they swore that no such person had been admitted.'

'It was all very mysterious, and we talked about it all the time over dinner, but it didn't begin to make me think of ghosts. The funny thing was that the telephone people hadn't booked us a call at that time, and couldn't remember anybody asking for a number.

'Well, we hadn't very long had dinner, when we heard a shriek upstairs, and I ran up to find the under-housemaid in a kind of fit.

'When at last I could get something out of her she told me that she'd gone into my wife's room to light the gas-fire, had heard somebody moaning and groaning behind her, and had beheld a strange lady with three eyes.

'The girl was in such in a state that I couldn't even laugh at the idea of a three-eyed lady. I tried to calm her down, but it was no use. She wouldn't spend another night in this house, and cleared out half an hour later.

'On the night following Mrs Eady, our cook—she is incidentally the wife of our butler—saw the three-eyed lady. She was made of sterner stuff than the housemaid, and although she ran away from the—the ghost or whatever it was, she's standing by us and was able to describe what she saw', I can corroborate her description, save for the three eyes of our uncanny visitor, for my wife and I have both seen her twice since. When we saw her we hadn't a very good view of her face, owing to the bad light, but I must admit that I saw nothing freakish about her. It was a big, fat woman in a yellow dress whom my wife and I saw cross the hall two nights later. We had only a glimpse of her, and my God! that was enough! She was obviously middle-aged, but her face was painted and her lips reddened, and her hair was that pale, artificial shade of gold which one connects with peroxide. The woman's make-up was a ghastly caricature of the spirit of coquetry. She was like a painted corpse, and she was moaning and heaving with sobs. We met her again four nights ago on the stairs, and we let her have the staircase to herself. According to Mrs Eady her third eye is in the middle of the base of her forehead, just above the other two.

'But meanwhile I'd seen twice more our gentleman visitor. Once he was standing at the telephone in my study, just as I'd first seen him. I braced myself and faced him, and he faced me with a kind of defiance. And I said,

'Who the devil are you, and what do you want?' Obviously I didn't say the right tiling. Apparently one shouldn't conjure that kind of visitor in those terms, although it seemed natural at the time. At the word "devil" his lips spread in a beastly grin, showing all his yellow teeth. His mouth stretched as if it were never going to stop. And then he uttered a hideous, obscene, neighing laugh. I don't mind owning that I didn't stay with him.

'A night or two later I returned to the dining-room about an hour after dinner, and there was he standing by the sideboard. He had a tumbler in his hand, if you please. Once more I cleared out and left him. My wife's seen him two or three times, and nearly died of fright. All our servants have seen one or both of them, and they've all cleared out, except the Eadys and the chauffeur, and he doesn't live in. The fact is that we're all being scared to death, and if you can do anything to help us, or suggest any remedy, we shall be eternally grateful to you.'

'I can suggest the remedy immediately,' said Chard, 'and that is exorcism. However, one likes to investigate these things and discover what they mean. By the way, I think you've left out one important detail. Didn't you tell me this morning that Mrs Scottman and yourself have lately been hearing explosions like pistol shots?'

Scottman nodded in the act of lighting a cigarette.

'Yes,' he said, 'two in quick succession. Generally at about dinner time, and the sounds seem to come from this very room. We've never managed to explain them away.'

Chard inclined his head.

'Now think, Mr Scottman,' he said. 'Is there any detail you have omitted? Just give your mind free play. Don't be afraid of drawing unconsciously on your imagination. You won't do that purposely, I know. Just try to think.'

Scottman raised his eyes, and there was silence for a few moments.

'One thing, when I was in the presence of the—the man,' he said at last,

'I seemed to notice something—a sort of faint, impure smell of stale spirits—as if somebody in the room were soused in bad whisky'

'Thank you,' said Chard quickly, 'and now tomorrow I shall want an interview with Mr Gallop. I suppose he's on the telephone. I wonder if you'd mind ringing up and asking when it would be convenient for me to call.'

Scottman rose, went to the telephone and spoke. Presently we heard him say, 'Is Mr Gallop in? . . . Oh, gone out for the evening? . . . Well, when he comes back will you please ask him to ring up Thames-side double nine double eight? Thank you.'

He hung up the receiver, and in the same instant the door was pushed open and a little dark lady, to whom we were subsequently introduced as Mrs Scottman, entered the room. We talked for five or six minutes until the rattling of a gong in the hall warned us that it was time to go up and dress. Scottman showed Chard and myself to our rooms, which were comfortably adjacent. I am fairly quick at getting into a boiled shirt and 'blacks', and I was the first to go downstairs. I did not know which was the drawing-room, and I had certain craven reasons for not wanting to explore the house alone, so I returned to the study, of which the door was open and the lights still burning.

No sooner was I in the room than the telephone bell began to buzz. As I was the only person on the spot it was clearly my duty to take down the receiver and bid the caller hold the line while I fetched my host and hostess. Besides, I had the idea that it might be the Mr Gallop whom Chard was so anxious to meet.

'Hullo!' I said.

'Thames-side double nine double eight?' asked a distant voice.

'Yes.'

'May I speak to Mr Bastow?'

'I don't know the name. This is Mr Scottman's house, and I'm a visitor here. But I can make enquiries.'

'Never mind,' came back the voice. 'I'm in a hurry. I expect it's all right. Would you mind taking a message? Tell Mr Bastow I haven't got his name on my books, and if it's a case of buying San Analdo Rails it's hopeless. They're still going up like rockets. If it's a case of selling I can deal with him. By the way, perhaps you wouldn't mind asking him to let me know if he's any relation to the other Bastow whom I used to deal with?'

'Which other Bastow?' something prompted me to ask.

'Oh, you remember. The Bastow. The man who came a cropper over San Analdos four years ago. He shot his wife afterwards, and blew out his own brains down in Surbiton. '

My head began to swim.

'Look here,' I exclaimed, 'do you mind telling me who's speaking and what it's all about?'

I heard 'Kindersham' and then 'stock-broker'. Then the voice grew clearer. 'I've just got home and found a message scribbled on my desk—"Thames-side double nine double eight, Bastow, San Analdo Rails."

Give him my message will you, please, and ask him to come and see me if he wants to sell. Can't wait. Goodbye.'

I hung up the receiver like a man in a dream. I knew there was nobody named Bastow in the house, and in the circumstances it was quite extraordinary to hear that a man of that name had shot his wife and then himself 'down in Surbiton' four years ago. As I turned away my gaze was bent downwards, but a sudden sensation that I had company in the room with me caused me to raise my eyes.

Standing between me and the door, in the full glare of the electric light, was a big, stout woman in an apricot-coloured dress. She must have been more than fifty, but her cheeks were heavily rouged, her lips painted, and her eyebrow's darkened. Her hair was a pale, unnatural gold and coiled in artificial curls. She would have been a sickening enough sight if she were honest flesh and blood, but I knew in my heart that she was not, and that she was something unholy and impure from another world beyond our ken. Her painted mouth was awry in an agony of weeping, and her shoulders rocked with sobbing. For one indescribable moment I looked into her face, and I saw' that which two of the servants had mistaken for a third eye.

... I don't know how I passed her, but I managed it somehow. I found myself out in the hall and running. Then a door got in my way and I flung it open. I turned on lights, and found myself in the drawing-room.

Presently the others came in, and I realised that my face could deceive nobody. I had wanted to spare Mrs Scottman, but she was quite calm and plucky about it. 'Besides,' she said, 'I've seen it too!'

So I told them all, and presently Chard asked me, 'I suppose you recognised what the two servants mistook for a third eye?'

I nodded and told them what I knew. No old soldier is going to make a mistake about a bullet-hole. And then I told them about the mysterious telephone call, and neither our host nor hostess had heard the name Bastow.

'Anybody know anything about San Analdo Rails?' Chard asked later over the dinner table.

'I only wish I had some,' Scottman replied. 'They're going up like wildfire, and they were ten a penny a few weeks ago. There was a boom in them four or five years ago, when a lot of the clever brigade burned their fingers.

'It happened that big mineral fields were supposed to be going to be opened in San Analdo, which is a tiny South American republic, and that sent up the price of the railway shares. And then there came a hitch over concessions, and down went the shares again. Concessions have just been granted, and the shares are roaring again, so those who held on to them are all right. But a lot of people went broke the first time—the inveterate gamblers in shares who go all out for a supposed good thing.'

We were halfway through dinner when a muffled explosion echoed through the house. It was quickly followed by another. Without a word of apology Chard sprang up and ran from the room, leaving us sitting still and staring. We heard him running down the hall towards the study.

He was back again at the end of two or three minutes, and his face was white and set.

'Seen anything?' Scottman asked just above a whisper.

Chard sat down heavily.

'Yes,' he said, 'I've seen him. I was right. There is only one thing to be done with this house, and that is exorcism. As to the cause of these phenomena, I think I know it already, and it just remains for Mr Gallop to confirm it. Tomorrow I think I can arrange for somebody to come here who will bring peace to your house again, but tonight if I were you I should go out to an hotel.'

Chard had an appointment with Gallop on the following evening, and took me along with him.

'Leave me to do the talking,' he said, 'and don't be surprised at anything I may say. Gallop may not be the type of man to open his heart if he thinks we are merely trying to gratify idle curiosity. '

Mr Gallop and his wife lived in a palatial house on Wimbledon Common. He was undersized and grey, and wore a waxed moustache. He was typical of a certain sort of City men, and he was one of those foul people who address perfect strangers as 'ole man' and 'ole chap' in an atrocious Cockney accent. He received us in a room which contained so many pictures that the wallpaper hardly had a chance.

'Mr Torrance and I,' said Chard, 'have been over in the States since 1920. Of course we heard the sad news about our friends the Bastows. But we never learned exactly how and why it happened, so we ventured to call. I daresay it will be very painful to you'

'If you was friends of old Sam Bastow,' Gallop interrupted suspiciously,

'It's funny I never met either of you before.'

'That has been our misfortune, but it is remedied at last.'

'That's all right, ole chap,' said Gallop. 'Your word's good enough for me. Well, I can tell you wot 'appened easily enough. Poor ole Sam got stung over San Analdos four years ago. You knew ole Sam? He had 'is ups and downs, and made money in 'is time, and he knew how to spend it too.

Lovely 'ouse at Chertsey, he had. Very often he sailed pretty close to the wind, but never mind about that. We've all got to make money, 'aven't we? When 'e gambled 'e didn't half gamble, and he thought nothing of having all his eggs in one basket. He had the tip about San Analdos, but he didn't get the best of the market, and as soon as he touched 'em down they flopped.

'And down he flopped too, and he went bust, and not for the first time. Only this time it looked as if it might be a prison job. There was certain things I needn't talk about—you understand, ole chap?

'Well, ole Sam and his missus 'ad to give up their 'ouse, so we asked 'em to come and stay with us. We'd always been pals, see? So they come, and—well, you know ole Sam 'ad never been a teetotaller. Liked 'is drop of juice, did Sam. And the worry he'd been through didn't 'elp to keep 'im off it. He caned my whisky properly, I can tell you.

'And then, well, one night at eight o'clock the missus and I heard two bangs. And I runs into the room at the back of the hall, and there was a nice scene, I give yer my word. He'd shot his missis straight through the forehead and blown out his own brains. Poor ole Sam! O' course, he was mad at the time. The coroner said so. And I didn't think it was quite playin' the game to go and do it in my 'ome. But when a man gets like that you never know wot he'll do. Mrs Gallop and me were never comfortable somehow in the 'ouse afterwards, and after about a year I sold it.

'That's all I can tell you, roughly. I s'pose he couldn't bear the thought of bein' pore. And look where San Analdos are today, if he'd only been able to hang on. Wonder what he'd think if he knew!'

'Perhaps he does know!' Chard said briefly.

And having thanked Mr Gallop and refused his hospitality—which took the form of strong waters—we left very shortly afterwards.

'Yes,' said Chard to me a little later, 'Bastow knows all right, and that's part of his punishment. You can guess the type he was from our friend Gallop—birds of a feather, you know—the type that only lives for money. And now San Analdos would have made them rich, but for his crowning act of folly and crime those two lost souls are tortured into giving the manifestations which we have both witnessed.

'Bastow's often seen at the telephone, because now he's trying to sell his beastly shares. In one case he seems to have established communication with somebody. At least, some servant seems to have left a message on a stockbroker's table. I've just arranged for a priest to go down to Scottman's house and see what he can do. Meanwhile, the whole affair is too beastly; let's do our best to forget it for the present.'

The Soldier

When Mr Lionel Danson retired from his activities in the City, he bought the attractive little property called Vailings, which is situated on the south side of Minthaven. Minthaven stands on the Hampshire coast, and looks across at the Needles, over the western entrance to the Solent. Mr Danson liked ships, and he was gratified by the spectacle of giant liners on their way to and from Southampton. These were visible from any of the upper windows on the south side of the house, and in order to have a more perfect view Mr Danson purchased a powerful telescope.

The house called Vailings was a converted farmhouse, with some seven acres of land attached to it. It stood beside the road leading straight down to the sea, and the first of the few buildings between Mr Danson's residence and the shingle beach was his own gardener's cottage, which stood about a hundred yards up the road and at the end of his own garden.

Mr Danson kept two indoor servants, and he also required a gardener whose wife could do some of the family washing and assist with some of the rough housework. A suitable couple named Wratham was discovered in Lymington, and they were promptly engaged and installed in the cottage. The Wrathams were not Hampshire people. Indeed, they seemed to have been in most parts of the country since the war, but despite the number of their situations their references were all excellent. Mrs Wratham was white and neurotic and not very strong, but otherwise they were a perfect couple for Mr Danson's needs.

Mr Danson had been comfortably settled in his new home some three months, and was preparing for bed one night, when he heard loud blasts from a siren. Looking out of his window he beheld the dark shape, gemmed with a thousand lights, of a great liner, homeward bound, gliding up the Solent. It happened to be a perfect moonlight night, so Mr Danson reached immediately for his telescope.

It was a large glass and clumsy to handle, and Mr Danson had not yet acquired skill in focussing an object quickly. Thus the road in front of the gardener's cottage was brought, it seemed, within a yard of his eyes, so that he could have counted every pebble. And then, as he shifted the focus, he saw something which caused him to forget all about the liner.

He kept vigil for part of the next three nights, and what he saw at close quarters and with his naked eyes sent him to town to see Francis Chard. I was with Chard at the time and heard his story.

Lionel Danson was a short, stoutish man in the fifties, and belonged to the happy type which normally lives well and worries about nothing. He gave me the impression of being a good fellow, and at ordinary times, I daresay he would have been the best of company. But just now he was pale and worried, for sufficiently good reasons. Let me tell in his own words what he saw through the telescope.

'I wasn't astonished, for the first moment or two, when I saw that the man was a soldier. Two or three families in the village have sons in the Army who come home on furlough. But I certainly wondered why he was wearing a shrapnel helmet and what he could want with the Wrathams. Then I must have given the screw some slight adjustment, and every ghastly detail of him blazed upon my eyes. Remember it was bright moonlight, and the telescope seemed to bring him within a yard of me. I saw a small roadside weed at his feet shivering in the night air.'

Danson paused. It was as if he could not bring himself to come straight to the gist of what he had to tell us.

'The gardener's cottage,' he continued, 'stands flush with the road. There is no garden in front and no path. As the road leads straight to the sea, it carries very little traffic, and I suppose a path would be superfluous. Well, he—it was standing before the door of the cottage and seemed to be knocking at it. '

He broke off abruptly, and Chard said, 'Perhaps you had better have a whiskey and soda?'

Danson smiled weakly.

'Thanks. Perhaps I had, if you don't mind. You'll think I'm an idiot, I know, but you'll remember that I saw him afterwards as close as I am to you. '

He drank the contents of the tumbler, which Chard presently brought him, at a single gulp. Then he resumed.

'He was a big fellow. I couldn't guess his age, because the face I saw in profile was the grey face of a corpse. His left side was turned to me, and he knocked on the door with his right hand. He could not have knocked with the left because he had none. The sleeve hung down, ragged and empty, and I saw a slow, steady drip of blood.

'His stained and faded khaki tunic was slightly powdered with something that looked like snow, and blackened with something that looked like soot. He was wearing leather equipment, but he was not in full kit. His bayonet scabbard was empty, and his haversack, instead of hanging over it, was on his back in place of a pack, with something rolled up underneath it.' Chard nodded. 'That would be a ground-sheet,' he said. 'He was in what we used to call "battle order".'

'I can remember all these details perfectly,' Danson continued, 'because his appearance was such a shock to me that a complete picture of him immediately impressed itself on my mind.'

'The more details the better,' said Chard. 'You couldn't by any chance see his numerals? I mean, what regiment did he belong to?'

'I don't know. But on his shoulder was a narrow strip of faded yellow ibbon, and underneath it, on the top of his sleeve, was a little red square, but inverted so that its angles pointed up and down and left and right. There was no mud on his boots and putties, but they looked wet. He had no rifle with him.

'The telescope shook so in my hands that I kept missing him, but I must have watched him off and on for several minutes. Not once did he move from his position, but stood there staring at an upper window and beating upon the door with his one fist. And suddenly he went—I don't know where. Just for a fraction of a second my unsteadiness of hand caused me to miss him with the telescope, and when I focussed it once more on the spot he was gone. There was only the empty road, and the same roadside weeds fluttering in the breeze.

'Well, Mr Chard, I went to bed feeling like nothing else on earth, and when I woke up in broad sunlight I tried to persuade myself that I'd dreamed or imagined the whole beastly business. But I knew I hadn't. I knew I had seen something which is commonly called a ghost, and I knew that it must have been the ghost of a soldier killed in the late war. I said nothing to my wife or to the Wrathams, but I started making inquiries in the village. Jokingly asked if there were a local ghost, you know, but nobody had heard of one. And then, beginning elsewhere, I asked who had been living in my cottage during the war. That was easily discovered. The couple are still in the village. They have three grown-up daughters, all married, but they never had a son; nor do they seem to have lost anyone very near and dear to them.

'The only thing to do, to satisfy myself—although I hated the idea—was to sit up and see if It came again. To cut my story as short as possible, It missed two nights. Then on the third night I focussed It once more in exactly the same spot, beating upon the door as before.

'I was ready and fully dressed, so I crept downstairs and out, and up the road. It was still there, facing the door, with Its back to the road. The blows on the door made only a faint muffled throbbing, which perhaps explained why the Wrathams did not hear and come down, to be confronted by the awful Thing which wanted to enter. I passed behind It with my heart thumping like an engine, went on up the road, and waited until I felt steadier. Then I turned and forced myself to go back, and for the first time I saw It from the other side.

'Mr Chard, I went right up to him and asked him what he wanted. Yes, I managed to do that. But the side on which I approached him was worse than the other. The breast of his tunic was blackened all over, and there was a great ragged hole in it. He took no notice of me. He did not even turn to look at me. But in that indescribable moment I felt myself fainting and reeling forward against that terrible Presence. I must have clutched at It to save myself, but I don't know if I touched anything. When I came to, I found myself lying face downwards on the road, and mercifully, alone.

'So now you will have guessed the cause of my visit. From what I have heard you would seem to be the only man able and willing to help me. I want to find rest for that poor soul who gave his body for his country, and I want to rid the neighbourhood of his terrifying presence. I don't know whether to tell the Wrathams or not. I would risk their thinking me a lunatic if it would do any good to tell them. The question is, whether it would be kinder to let them know and keep them in a state of apprehension or let them suddenly discover the horror for themselves.'

Chard considered, and glanced at me.

'That,' he said, 'is a point which we can decide later.'

Danson's pale face brightened a little.

'You mean,' he cried eagerly, 'that you will come down and help me.'

'Certainly,' Chard replied. 'We both will. Today, if you like.'

And so it befell that we accompanied Danson back to Hampshire, but before we started Chard and I had a private talk.

'Here's a very curious case,' Chard commented, 'pre-supposing that our friend Danson isn't a liar or a lunatic. Here's a soldier, evidently killed in the late war, haunting the outside of a cottage with which he apparently had no connection in life. What do you make of him so far, Torrance?'

'He was evidently killed by a shell,' I said, 'and probably his rifle was blown out of his hands at the same time. The black stuff on him must have been explosive, but I can't account for the white stuff unless it were snow. '

'But what do you make of that yellow strip on his shoulder and the red patch on top of his sleeve?'

'I'm coming to that,' I answered, 'and it's rather a coincidence that I should know. I believe the yellow slip indicates that he belonged to the Fourth —shires, who were in the 190th Brigade attached to the Naval Division. In that case the red patch would mean that he was in "A" Company. I happen to know, because my brother was a second loot in that very company, and was wearing the same strips and patches when I ran across him near Bapaume. Perhaps, if I write, he'll be able to help us.'

'Perhaps he will,' Chard agreed, 'when we get a little more data. Did he ever do any fighting in the snow, do you know?'

'Almost certain, I should think. There was plenty of snow about during both the winters he was out there. I'm glad I remembered his yellow strips and red patches. It's about the first time I've been able to give you any material help, Chard. '

We met Danson at Waterloo in the afternoon and caught a good train to Brockenhurst, where his car was garaged. He drove us the ten miles over a comer of the New Forest, through the western outskirts of Lymington, and down into Minthaven, which is at the head of a spear of dry land striking through marshes to the sea.

It was not a typical old-world seaside village. There was little to see, and nothing to interest the archaeologist: no crazy, dilapidated cottages leaning over cobbled streets in an odour of fish, tar and hemp. The place was open and scattered and wind-swept, and most of the buildings which took the eye were comparatively modem, but it had a charm of its own. Mrs Danson received us delightfully. The reason for our visit had been kept from her, and she took us to be friends of her husband and connected in some vague way with that mysterious thing called business. Danson showed us over the house and pointed out Mrs Wratham, who was helping in the kitchen. The house being old—the oldest in Minthaven— was sufficient excuse for our being shown into every room from attic to cellar.

We both glanced at her curiously. She was a woman in the early thirties, but her hair was already streaked with grey. She looked wan and worried, and moved about with an air of lassitude. She gave me the impression of being literally tired of life.

Danson took us to the window of his room from which he had first seen the apparition. The road ran by on our right on the flank of Danson's long garden, with a low hedge between. Beyond the hedge stood the Wrathams' cottage, and Danson let us see, by lending us the telescope, how plainly he must have seen that which stood outside the door.

While Chard was looking through the telescope, the door of the cottage actually opened, and a short, thick-set man of about forty, emerged.

'That's Wratham,' said Danson, and Chard involuntarily craned a little forward.

The man did not look in the direction of the house, but turned and slouched away in the direction of the sea. Chard laid aside the glass.

'Where's he off to?' my friend inquired. 'I'd like to have a word with him. '

'Well, he knocked off work about an hour ago, and I suppose by this time he's had his tea, and is off to drink a pint of beer at the Cannon.'

'That, I suppose, is the village pub,' said Chard. 'There's only the one road, so we can't miss it. Mind if we go down and have a word with him?'

'Just as you like,' Danson replied, good-humouredly; and Chard and I got our hats and sallied forth.

The Cannon Inn was about a quarter of a mile distant and within two hundred yards of the sea. We walked into the sand-strewn tap-room, where half-a-dozen working men were gathered around the shove-ha'penny board in the window. Wratham was easily identified. He stood aloft at a comer of the counter, with a pint glass of brown ale half empty at his elbow. He looked surly and moody, his eyes were red-rimmed and there was a droop to his mouth. Chard ordered drinks for everybody in the room.

The group around the shove-ha'penny board split up as the men came shyly up to the counter to take the hastily filled glasses. Chard selected a youngish fair-haired, good-looking fellow and tapped him on the chest.

'Hullo!' he exclaimed. 'Weren't you with me in the Fourth—shires?'

The other grinned and shook his head.

'No, zur. I was in the Artillery.'

'Well, then, you've got a double, or, rather, you had one. I thought for a moment I'd seen a ghost. Anybody here believe in ghosts?'

He looked around the room and laughed, and everybody laughed too except Wratham. He glowered, finished his beer, wiped his mouth on the back of his hand, and stared defiantly at Chard.

'Lot o' rot!' he grunted, and slouched out.

The other men were quick to apologise for his manners.

'He don't belong here, sir, and the quicker he be gone the better.' Chard laughed it off, and I could see that something had given him perfect satisfaction.

On the way back he said to me, 'The Wrathams know. I'm convinced of that. And the mere fact that they know and haven't said a word is enough for me. I think one short talk with that woman will clear up everything. But we may as well see the apparition if we can—to satisfy ourselves, you know.'

We could not use the window of Danson's room that night without arousing the curiosity of his wife, who slept next door; but overhead was an untenanted attic, and we kept watch at the window there with Danson's telescope.

It was a long vigil. Not until nearly half-past two did Chard's pose suddenly become rigid, and I heard him draw' a quick, harsh breath as if he had been touched by sudden cold. He remained quite still for nearly a minute; then, without a word, he passed the glass to me, and I focussed the road just in front of the Wratharn's cottage door.

I need not describe what I saw. That has been done already in Danson's words, and I have nothing to add. I had seen sights like that on the battlefield, but never broken men standing upright as this apparition of a broken man was standing. I did not look at it very long.

'You're not going—up the road, are you?' I asked falteringly, of Chard.

'I don't see the need,' Chard replied, with a catch in his voice. Neither did I.

On the following moming, soon after Wratham had started work in Danson's garden, Chard and I walked up to the cottage and knocked. Mrs Wratham opened the door to us.

'We want to speak to you, Mrs Wratham,' Chard said solemnly.

The little white-faced woman stared at us in mingled curiosity and alarm. But she asked us in, and we followed her into the little kitchen where clothes were airing in front of the range.

'Mrs Wratham,' said Chard very quietly, 'who is the soldier who comes and knocks upon your door—the poor, dead, mangled soldier?'

For answer she uttered a faint scream and clapped her hands to her eyes. In a moment I saw the tears running down under her palms.

'Don't be afraid,' said Chard gently, 'it would be better for you to tell us.' She calmed herself and faced us half defiantly.

'He is a ghost,' she said. 'There are such things as ghosts, you know.'

'I know. I know. But tell us who he was.'

'He was my first husband,' she answered, drying her eyes and beginning to talk in a dreary monotone. 'So he's found us out and followed us here? I knew he would. He's followed us everywhere. Isn't there any peace for the sinful—even in this world?

'His name was Martin, and he was in the—shires. I married him when he was home on leave. I was only a girl then. And he went back to the trenches and left me, and I was lonely. It seemed to me when he was gone that I hadn't loved him like I thought I had. And then Wratham came along.

'Wratham was cattle man on a farm, so they didn't make him go and fight. He spent his nights in my cottage, and nobody knew. I meant to marry him if anything happened to Tom. There'd been heavy fighting all round Cambrai' (she pronounced it Cambria) 'where Tom was, but he seemed to have come through it safe.

'And then one night at the end of 1917—it was the night before New Year's Eve—Wratham woke me up and said as there was somebody knocking at the door. A quiet, muffled sound it was. And we was frightened that he'd come home on leave, so it was me that had to go down. And it was Tom Martin sure enough, but not as I'd ever seen him before, all bloody and grimed with his eyes full of sorrow and anger. And I knew 'twas his spirit and that he'd just been killed, and I gave one loud cry and fainted.

'Since then he's never let us alone for long, although we've moved here, there, and everywhere. Wratham's clever at lots of things, and he can get work anywhere. But as soon as we're settled in a place Tom Martin finds us out and comes knocking at our door of a night, and we have to move on somewhere else. We've had no peace for eight years, and the terror of it is wearing me to skin and bone. Once we got a clergyman to come and pray, but it didn't do no good. The only way for us is to end it all, and I think it will come to that at last.'

And, rather to my surprise, Chard had no comfort to offer her.

'I thought from the beginning,' he said to me as we walked back, 'that the Wrathams might be responsible for the phenomena. You see, nothing had been seen until they took over the cottage. And when I saw them I knew that they knew, and I wondered why they hadn't told. The fact that nobody in the village had belonged to the—er—the dead man's regiment made me quite certain. There's only one thing for friend Danson to do, and that is to get rid of the Wrathams.'

'Poor devils!' I exclaimed. 'Can't anything be done for them?'

Chard shrugged his shoulders.

'I don't know what,' he said. 'This isn't a case of a haunted house—it's a case of a haunted couple. It might be dangerous to try to interfere. We've got to pay for our sins—in some way or another, you know.'

I shuddered. A few minutes since it had been a warm, sunny morning, but now the wind seemed very cold.

A week later I had an answer to the letter which I presently addressed to my brother. Here is an extract:

Yes, I remember Tom Martin very well, probably because he was always panicking for leave because he suspected that his wife wasn't being faithful to him. Of course, we couldn't even send the application up to Brigade. There was too much of that sort of thing, and besides the man seemed to have no real grounds for his suspicion.

I shan't forget the morning when he was killed. It was on December the thirtieth, and there'd been snow on the ground for weeks. Everything had been suspiciously quiet for a long time, and on that morning Jerry came over in the snow, camouflaged in white smocks, and pinched part of our front line on Welsh Ridge without a shot being fired. We were in support at the time and the first we knew of it was the barrage he put over to try to stop us from counter-attacking. Of course, we had to go up and dig him out, and the communication trench (called Central Avenue) was one of the warmest places through which I ever passed.

That was where Martin was killed. A whizz-bang dropped on top of the traverse right in front of him, and the ground being iron-hard, he hadn't a chance. I remember writing a letter of condolence to his wife, and wondering all the while if there was anything in the poor chap's suspicions.

'That,' said Chard grimly, 'is a matter on which you can assuage his curiosity—at your own discretion. '

The Tryst

I was playing bridge at the club one afternoon, when Chard came in quietly and sat down beside me. We were all engrossed, and I was engaged in trying to make two no trumps out of my own good hand and my partner's bad one, so I did no more than nod to him when he came in. I just got my call, which put me on level terms with our opponents at one game all; but at the next deal they made a little slam in spades, and the arithmetic began I passed fifty shillings, the price of three lost rubbers, over to the man on my right, and vowed to give up the game. I am always saying that, but I still go on playing. We four players and Chard were the only people in the card-room, and after money had changed hands my late partner rose to go. Chard was invited to cut in, but he refused. The other two, seeing that bridge was done with for the time being, rose and talked themselves slowly out of the room. I sat on, because I had an idea that Chard wanted to talk to me.

I was right. He drew up his chair alongside mine, helped himself to my cigarettes, which lay on a comer of the card-table, and began in a subdued tone, 'I've had something happen which may interest you. Alma Lemaitre has been to see me.'

'Bad lad!' I laughed.

The woman was still young, but quite notorious. She was a celebrated beauty of the type which used to thrive on the picture postcard trade. She could dance a little, sing a little, and act a little, and she was a popular favourite in musical comedy and revue. She must have made a great deal of money, but not enough to satisfy her vanity and greed and her vulgar hankerings after display. Half-a-dozen well-known men of the day had been her lovers, and I don't know how many wealthy nonentities besides.

'She interested me,' Chard continued. 'Do you remember the old tale of the Lyttleton ghost?'

'Oh, yes. Where the lady came and warned him—'

'That's right. Well, Alma Lemaitre's had a similar warning, or thinks she has. She's in a pretty bad state. That's why she came to me. By the way, do you happen to remember Lord John Rompton shooting himself last year?'

'What, that poor lad at Oxford? Yes.'

'I didn't know until today that Alma was the cause of that.'

I turned to stare at Chard. 'Was she? Did she tell you so?'

'Not in so many words, but the inference was quite obvious. She knew him well, it seems. I suppose he thought she was straight and fell madly in love with her, and afterwards discovered that he wasn't the only pebble on the beach. But I'd better tell you just what happened.

'She made an appointment with me on the phone and then came round.

'She isn't playing anywhere now, which is perhaps as well. She's a strange creature, Torrance. Temperament without any genius, essentially common, beautiful in a certain cheap and showy way, and with a certain sex appeal. Quite conscienceless and terribly ignorant, of course. She doesn't believe in God, but she believes in mascots. She doesn't believe in any hereafter, but now she believes in ghosts. She's all contradictions and superstitions.

'Well, she came to me shaking all over and nearly crying, begging me to believe her story and to help her. It seems that she was awakened from sleep last night and couldn't think what had awakened her. She had a vague sense of terror which grew and grew. Then she felt her gaze being attracted to a far comer of the room where she saw a faint, bluish light which gradually assumed the shape of a man; and suddenly she recognised Lord John

Rompton, who had been dead a year. "I used to know Johnny very well," she explained to me naively. "I didn't mean to do him any harm—I swear I didn't. It knocked me right over when I heard what he'd done."

'Well, it seems she was frozen stiff with terror. She couldn't move or cry out. And the apparition came right up to the bed and stood beside her. Having looked at her long and fixedly, it said, "On Saturday at midnight I shall come to fetch you." And then, to use her own words, it faded away. And that, Torrance, is all the story. That she believes it herself is beyond doubt, and she came to me begging me to do something to drive the ghost away and save her life.'

I turned it all over in my mind.

'Well, what do you make of it?' I asked presently. 'Hallucination induced by a guilty conscience, bad dream, or an actual spirit manifestation?'

Chard shrugged his shoulders.

'My dear fellow, she hasn't a conscience of any sort, and I think it's long odds on it being a bad dream. But on the other hand, you know, it mightn't be. Of course, we can't really do anything except give her comfort and confidence, and it would be uncharitable to say the least, to withhold those. So I said I'd do what I could. She wants me to be with her when the time comes. Oh, and she wants us to go and dine with her at her flat tonight.'

'Who's keeping her now?' I asked doubtfully.

'I don't know, but he won't be there. She told me—rather pointedly, I thought—that she was alone, with only the servants. She's going to have her maid to sleep in the room for the next night or two. Well, what do you think?'

'I'll come and dine with pleasure,' I said. 'I should like to meet her. And I'll certainly join you and her on Saturday night. I don't suppose anything interesting will happen, though. At least, I hope it won't be anything tragic.'

'The only thing we can do,' said Chard, 'is to impress on her the probability that it was all a bad dream, or, failing that, assure her that ghosts are no more always able to carry out their threats than mortals are. I've done that already, and sent her off a little comforted. I believe it's quite possible for people to frighten themselves to death over an hallucination. '

I agreed. 'A great many believe that Lord Lyttleton of the ghost story did that, although he boasted that he would "bilk the ghost".'

Chard smiled and rose.

'Well,' he said, 'come round for me at about half-past seven.'

At half-past seven I duly called for him, and we went in a taxi to the street off Park Lane where Alma Lemaitre lived in a block of large mansions.

She was in better fettle than I had expected to see her when she received us, but it did not take me long to discover the reason. She had flown to the bottle for comfort, and not altogether in vain. She shook us warmly by the hands and thanked us at great length for coming. There was something pathetic in the sight of this creature, who was capable of none of the higher emotions, trying to conjure up gratitude.

I suppose Alma Lemaitre was then about twenty-seven, and there was no doubt at all as to her showy beauty. Her complexion was so skilfully laid on that it was hard to believe that it was artificial. Her hair was cleverly kept very fair and she was beautifully gowned in the exact shade of blue which matched her eyes.

We were shown first into a large drawing-room, really magnificently furnished, which would not have been in bad taste but for a latent air of trying to overwhelm the visitor. Everything was just a little too sumptuous and over-done. And there were too many—far too many—photographs of men in expensive frames.

When we were all seated she rose and brought one of these photographs over to show us.

'That's Johnny,' she said.

I looked at the likeness of a boy of twenty, who had a small head, a weak aristocratic face, and an air of having at some time outgrown his strength. There was nothing terrifying in the sight of this weedy youth, whose head and narrow shoulders somehow suggested that he was well above the average height.

'I suppose,' said Alma to me, 'Mr Chard's already told you?'

'About what you thought you saw?'

Her face twitched nervously.

'You can cut that right out,' she said. 'It's no use arguing with me. I did see Johnny last night, and I did hear him talk. It's no use telling me that I dreamed it. I know perfectly well when I'm dreaming. And it's no use telling me that I imagined it. I don't imagine things. And I wasn't blotto either. Do you think I wouldn't believe that I dreamed it or imagined it if I could? Do you think I want to believe that I saw a ghost and heard him say that he was going to fetch me away on Saturday night? No, it's true—it's gospel truth. And you gentlemen, who've seen ghosts before, and know all about them, you're not going to let him do it, are you?'

'That's all right,' said Chard soothingly. 'Don't you worry any more, Miss Lemaitre. We shall be with you. Just leave everything to us.'

The gong sounded then and we went in to dinner. In the presence of the two maids who waited at table we could not discuss the late Lord John Rompton or his wraith; and it was a little difficult at first to find common ground with Alma.

I must say she gave us an extraordinarily good dinner. Since her rise in the world she had learned, among other things, a great deal about food. I suspected that the dinner had been sent in from somewhere, it was so perfectly cooked and served. And the Verve Cliquot floating on molten ice in silver buckets—to which Alma allowed herself to be helped unstintedly—was beyond reproach.

I found the poor frightened little harlot extremely interesting as a study.

With all her shallowness and lack of brains she had achieved her ambition—such as it was—and that is something more than generally falls to the lot of the deep and shrewd. She had acquired some of the more obvious manners of a lady, but wore them with an air of being in fancy dress. Her voice affected culture. The pitch was right, and the vowels were pure enough. But one knew instinctively that she had learned only recently to speak correctly, and I wondered what her natural accents would be like. I did not know that I was ever to hear them.

After dinner we followed her into the drawing-room, and there she unbosomed herself to some extent on the subject of Lord John Rompton.

'I don't see why he wanted to bear me a grudge. He said it was my fault. He said it in a letter which he left behind. That got hushed up. His people wanted it hushed up, and so did I; so it didn't get into the papers.

'I admit I was friends with him at first. He was quite a nice boy, and a lord's a lord. But I didn't want him for a lover. There was somebody else, you see. Besides, we couldn't afford each other. He'd got no money. His father, the Marquis, took care of that. I'd have married him, of course, if the old man had been reasonable. But as things were it could be neither one thing nor the other. I tried to make him see it all sensibly, but he wouldn't. And I couldn't have him always here, because somebody else, that I couldn't afford to quarrel with, would have been jealous. And then he went and did—that.'

I thought of a Spanish proverb—'It is a dreadful thing to love a prostitute'—and I was sorry for the poor lad. I was sorry for her too, for I could imagine her early home-life and upbringing. What chance had she ever had, with her good looks as her only asset, which made her tum naturally to the highest bidder? All her capacity for honest love had probably been crushed out of her by the first man who bought her acquiescence. She was now no more than the husk of a woman. If her experience were a fact, and not a dream, there could be little soul left for that other spirit to take with it to the place whence it came.

We stayed with her until after midnight, for she dreaded being left. Her parting words were, 'You'll come round early on Saturday night, won't you? Come to dinner again. And afterwards we'll play a game of cards or something. I'll let you go directly after twelve if nothing happens.'

That was on Thursday night, or, to be precise, Friday morning.

I shall not forget that Saturday night until the day of my death. As before, we were the only guests. I am sure that we—or perhaps it was only Chard—inspired her with confidence. I expected to find her more highly strung than on the previous occasion, but she was not so at first. The impression made by the visitation had begun to wear off, and her natural agnosticism had had time to grapple with it.

So the meal was a cheerful one, and we did not at first refer to the object of our visit.

But I was far from comfortable, and so, I learned afterwards, was Chard.

We both knew that if the thing she had seen and heard were not bred by her own imagination, but a malignant spirit which had uttered a purposeful menace, we were powerless to help her.

A big clock ticked on the mantelshelf in the drawing-room, and when we entered the room after dinner my gaze involuntarily strayed in its direction.

It was then eight minutes past nine, and Alma, reading my thought, said,

'It's exactly right. I put it on by Big Ben.'

I saw Chard's face fall. We had both set our watches fast by a few minutes, so that we might show her and deceive her into thinking that she was safely past midnight before the hour had actually stuck. Surreptitiously I set mine right again.

We had nearly three hours to wait and it was during those three hours that the strain began to tell on the wretched woman, indeed on all of us.

She asked if we played poker, and, learning that we did, she got out card-table and cards, and we proceeded to play a dull game for small stakes.

'Three' poker is not very interesting, but apart from the natural dullness of the game there was the dreadful atmosphere of a condemned cell. I felt as if I were helping to distract the thoughts of somebody waiting to be hanged, to while away the last dreadful hours of a doomed life.

Alma won a little money from both of us, and we were glad to lose to her. I began to hope that we might be able to take her safely past midnight without her noticing the time. But it was a vain hope, for I saw her gaze straying more and more often in the direction of the clock as time wore on.

And when at last it struck half-past eleven she suddenly dropped her cards, leaned her elbows on the table, and burst into tears.

'It's no use,' she wailed. 'I can't go on playing. He's coming for me in half an hour. I know he is. I didn't really believe it a little while ago. But I do now. I can feel it. He's coming for me.'

'Oh, nonsense,' said Chard, rising and laying a hand lightly on her back.

'You mustn't think that. You help him if you think that, you know.'

But for two or three minutes she refused to be comforted. Chard glanced at me and looked meaningly at the decanter of whisky. I poured out a stiff tot for Alma, which she drank almost at a gulp. It seemed to brighten her, and she ceased crying.

'Let's have another round of jackpots,' I suggested.

But she shook her head.

'Really, I can't go on playing. Can't fix my mind. Do you mind if we sit and talk? Talk to me all the time. I want to stop thinking if I can.'

Chard and I did our best, but it was hard to manufacture conversation.

During one hiatus Alma smiled wanly, and said that it was like waiting at the dentist's, only much worse.

'I want you,' she added, 'when it's twelve o'clock to come and sit each side of me and hold my hands. I shan't feel afraid then.'

The minutes dragged horribly. The ticking of the clock was like a pulse of fear beating through the room. I don't know how a man condemned to death endures his last minutes, nor do I know how those who sit with him endure them. In our case we had Hope, but with Hope there goes always her ugly sister who is called Suspense.

At five minutes to twelve I lit a cigarette, and I smoked it so furiously that I had thrown away the stub before midnight. I tried to reason against a choking sensation of terror which assailed me. Because this woman who deserved bad dreams had suffered one, why should we sit, twitching and anxious, waiting for its improbable fulfilment? I had come definitely to call it a dream now. I dared not imagine that it was anything else.

Chard was admirable. His calmness and his smiling demeanour, all assumed for Alma's sake, would have pacified a terrified child. When the clock rang the first stroke of twelve he turned to her with a confident smile.

'Well, here's zero hour,' he said. 'You're not afraid, are you?'

'Come and hold my hands,' said Alma shakily; and she stretched them out.

Truly, I hardly know how to write what followed. It was all so quick and so inexpressibly ghastly. No man's pen could do justice to the agonising horror of the things that happened. It is in my power to be no more than brief and plain.

I had an ash-tray on my knees, and was laying it aside on a small polished table preparatory to rising, when, without the least sound, or warning, the lights went out, plunging us all into utter darkness. At that moment of all moments the effect on me was such that I thought my heart had stopped; and Alma's scream, harsh and throaty, like a blast of an engine's whistle, sent another knife through my heart and entrails. Chard's voice broke in, steady and calm as ever.

'It's a short circuit,' he said. 'Don't be alarmed. Got a match, Torrance?'

I began frenziedly to fumble in my pockets. Something or somebody brushed past my knees in the dark.

'All right, Chard,' I cried out irritably, 'keep away from me. I'll find one in a minute. '

And Chard's voice answered from across the room.

'I haven't moved. Oh, my God, what's that?'

I heard the matches rattle in my pocket, but before my fingers had closed over the box there came another scream from Alma Lemaitre. And then, for the first and last time, I heard her speak in her natural, unaffected voice. It tore through the darkness like shrieking fragments of shell.

' 'Elp! 'Elp! Johnny, you damned cad! Take him away! Take 'im away!'

It ended in a kind of bubbling gasp, and then I struck a match and saw Alma lying on the floor at the foot of the chair on which she had been sitting. Chard ran to the electric light switch and turned the lights on again while I bent over her. There had been no short circuit.

I lifted Alma off the floor and Chard came hastening back to us. But we could do nothing. The heart of the painted woman, who rested in my arms with dread and damnation on her face, had already ceased to beat.

The Bungalow at Shammerton

There's a great deal to be said for Yoxall's point of view,' Chard remarked. 'At least he has saved all risk of prejudicing our minds. He says in effect, "I believe my bungalow is haunted, but I shan't tell you what by or how. Here are the keys. Go and see for yourself. If you suffer experiences similar to mine there is something radically wrong with the bungalow. If you don't then there is something radically wrong with me." Yes, I think he's right. Whatever happens will rule out altogether the theory of suggestion.'

'But one likes to know what one is up against,' I demurred.

'Something pretty unpleasant, I should say,' said Chard. 'Yoxall doesn't seem to be the kind of man to be scared lightly, and he said frankly that it was quite impossible for him to live in the bungalow until it has been—spiritually cleansed was, I think, the term he used.'

'How long has he had it?' I asked.

'About nine months, I think. But he's only just started trying to live in it. Those places aren't used in the winter, and he bought the place, lock, stock and barrel, at the end of last summer, when it was going cheap, from a man named Rushby. Who Rushby was, and whether he was scared out of the place, I don't pretend to know.'

'Shammerton used to be a pretty warm spot,' I said reflectively. 'It is now,' said Chard. 'Nearly all these little riverside colonies are hotbeds of immorality. Most of the bungalows are built for the purpose of illicit week-ends. Yoxall remarked that only about seven per cent of his neighbours were properly married, and he warned me not to take any notice of uproars in the middle of the night. Drunken orgies seem to be the rule rather than the exception. Also a celebrated comedian who honours the locality has a habit, when in his cups, of beating his wife, and her protests can be heard at least two miles down the river. '

'What you might call a really nice, select neighbourhood!' I remarked.

Yet Shammerton when we saw it in the afternoon sunlight looked beautiful and peaceful and good. The long river reaches were gay with small craft, manned for the most part by young fellows in immaculate flannels and pretty and gaily-dressed girls, who looked like their sisters or the sisters of their friends. Parasols sprang up here and there like brilliant fungi, and from nooks where the water was darkened by the shade of trees came the sound of laughter and the clink of teacups.

Our destination was on a peninsula beside a backwater, where a long arm of sluggish stream, fed by a rushing weir beside a lock, wandered for three-quarters of a mile before finding its way back to the parent river. This peninsula was, as Chard put it, 'all bungalows'. They stood at discreet intervals in pretty leafy gardens, each with its own landing-stage, to which were moored punts, skiffs, dinghies, and occasionally motor-launches. Most of these bungalows were charming to look at and whimsically named.

Ours—or rather Yoxall's—was called 'Munki Puz', because of a monkey puzzle which grew on the miniature lawn in front. For the rest it was like a cottage in a fairy play, and looked almost too good to be true. The little garden in front was like a bower of roses, and the wall and porch were covered with pink ramblers.

A charwoman who spent all her summers working in the bungalows received us as we entered and asked if she should make tea. She had received telegraphic instructions from Yoxall on the previous day to prepare the bungalow for our reception and to get in food.

'I've had a fire in every room,' she was careful to inform us, 'and aired all the beds, though you need not have been afraid of the place being damp at this time of the year.'

She seemed quite ignorant of the reason for our presence, and of the sinister reputation of the bungalow, but, of course, as it occurred to both of us, she was never there at night. She brewed tea for us, and then Chard told her that she might go as soon as she had laid our supper.

We had still four or five hours of daylight before us, and Yoxall's punt and dinghy lay invitingly at their moorings; so we loaded the punt with cushions and Chard steered us down the backwater and out into the river We lazed and smoked for an hour or so under a willow, and then glided on leisurably as far as Shammerton Bridge, where we landed for an hour and drank iced lager at the Swan Inn.

Both Chard and I were agreed that no house could have differed more widely in appearance than 'Munki Puz' from the conventional 'haunted house', which one is apt to picture when ghost stories are told. It was a typical riverside, week-end bungalow, pretty and cheerful, and vulgar as a grisette, furnished principally with fumed oak, and flaming with loud chintzes and cushions in primary colours. I think that this, and the fact that we did not know what to expect, lent both of us an additional interest in the case.

Chard's plan of campaign was purely negative.

'I think,' he said, 'we had better behave like ordinary people staying in the bungalow. Ordinary people don't sit up to see ghosts, and if there are any experiences to be had I don't think we shall miss them. Thus I think we'll go quietly off to bed at twelve o'clock, unless something has happened before then. I have respected Yoxall's wish that we should approach the case with perfectly open minds, and for that reason I haven't made any inquiries as to what has been happening in the bungalow. We can make inquiries afterwards. As the bungalow can't be more than fifteen years old we shan't have very much trouble in getting to learn all we want to know. '

'Evidently,' I said, 'the charwoman doesn't suspect anything.'

'I don't suppose anybody does. Yoxall wouldn't have told her, and as he didn't know any of his neighbours, he wouldn't have told them. I don't know if the previous owner—Rushby, wasn't that his name?—was troubled in the same way or if'

He paused suddenly.

'Or if,' I suggested, 'the cause of the trouble took place in his time.'

'Exactly,' said Chard. 'But we needn't begin to speculate about that yet.'

We returned up stream at sunset and reached 'Munki Puz' just as the long shadows were merging into dusk. I had the keys, and having opened the front door, I preceded Chard into the dining-room and paused on the threshold to savour the atmosphere.

'Filthy stink in here,' I remarked. 'I wonder where it comes from.'

'What sort of stink?' Chard enquired.

'Sort of river smell.'

'That's not astonishing in a river-side bungalow.'

'But the room's been shut up, and there's no smell outside.'

Chard came beside me and stood sniffing for a moment.

'Hum!' he said briefly. 'I think we'll have the windows open.'

It was a stale, green, damp smell, suggestive of stagnant river water and rotten weed. It soon passed, however, in the draught which we caused to blow through the room, and we sat down to our cold chicken and ham and salad. But somehow we were neither happy nor comfortable. I could not help wondering how that foul river smell had come to be imprisoned in the room, and I knew that Chard's mind was busy with the same unprofitable speculations.

'We may as well sit out in the garden,' said Chard, when we had both finished eating. 'I see there are seats, and it will be much pleasanter there.'

So in late twilight we drew deck-chairs to the edge of the backwater, lit our pipes, and proceeded to enjoy the warmth and beauty of the scented night.

From all around us strains of music stole out of the distance. There must have been a gramophone in every bungalow, and a loud-speaker in most. With these sounds mingled the steady, forceful, monotonous music of the weir. In many of the gardens Chinese lanterns were alight, and a spurious atmosphere of peace and beauty seemed to brood over our surroundings, as if we had strayed into some sort of vicious fairyland. To add colour to the Illusion certain sinister sounds were borne to us out of the far distance, hideous cachinnations of drunken mirth, and laughter of a besotted idiot. Fish were rising in the backwater at our feet. A fat old chub under the far bank rolled and wallowed after the flies that dropped on to the water. I suppose we were both subconsciously waiting for something, and then suddenly there came a heavier splash at the base of some rushes twenty yards away. I started violently, and heard Chard's chair wince under his sudden movement.

'What was that?' I asked.

'Otter, I expect,' said Chard.

'Never heard of otters in this part of the river,' I remarked uneasily. And then next moment there glided slowly into view a punt propelled by a short, stout young man in flannels. Two young women, obviously 'river girls' of the baser sort, reclined on cushions at his feet.

Manoeuvring his craft with easy skill, and taking no notice of us, he calmly made fast to our landing stage and stepped out. I saw then that he was obviously a young Jew.

He approached us at his leisure and gave us one nod of easy affability.

"'Ullo!' he said cheerfully. 'Where's Bert?'

Neither of us moved. Chard, lying on his back in the chair, regarded the young man with intense disfavour.

'Bert who?' he asked.

'Bert Rushby. You know ole Bert Rushby. Don't he live 'ere now?'

'I'm afraid he doesn't. Somebody of that name sold the bungalow last year to my friend, Mr Yoxall.'

'O-oh! I see. Sorry to 'ear that. I wanted to see Bert. Bert's a real sport.'

He winked and gave a backward glance at the punt. 'I got a couple of birds 'ere,' he added.

Neither of us spoke, and I was within an ace of laughing aloud. It was quite obvious that this unpleasant little cockney Jew had the effrontery to expect to be asked to bring his two doxies into the bungalow'. When something in our frozen manner penetrated his intelligence, but not his hide, he seemed vaguely aggrieved.

'I suppose you dunno where Bert's livin' nowadays?' he asked.

'Never met the man,' Chard replied frigidly.

'Eh? Oh, well, I wish 'e was 'ere now. Bert was a real sport. Never mind, we can go down to the Swan. So long!'

So saying, our visitor retreated in good order, stepped back into the punt, and at a minute's end he and his companions had vanished like a dream.

Then Chard burst out laughing.

'Quite typical of Shammerton I should think,' he said. 'Perfect stranger arrives with two of the local pets and expects to be entertained to a drunken orgy.'

'Sidelight, too, on Mr Rushby,' I remarked. 'He was a sport, you see.'

One easily gathered that filthy little cad's conception of the term. I wonder what has become of Mr Rushby. '

'Answers to the name of Bert,' Chard observed. 'Therefore shall he perish eternally.'

My mind began to dwell more than ever on Mr Rushby, and the more I thought, the more certain I became in my own mind that he was responsible for such 'hauntings' as took place in the bungalow. Where the impression came from I don't know, but I found it engraved in my mind with all the clarity and depth of certainty. And yet, so far as I knew, the man was still alive.

It was close on midnight when we returned to the house. There were two large bedrooms and one smaller one, and it was in the two large rooms that our beds had been made up. I had selected the one in front of the bungalow, and Chard was to sleep in the room behind.

At the moment of entering my bedroom, candle in hand, I was aware once more of that disgusting river smell, so I called Chard and threw open the French windows leading into the garden which we had just left.

'It's rather queer,' remarked Chard, looking up and down the room. 'I wonder if the smell is one of the phenomena we are supposed to investigate. And—this is a lot queerer still.'

He pointed at my bed. The clothes were rumpled, and at the end nearest the window the top blanket and sheet had been drawn aside, exactly as if the bed had lately been slept in and vacated. And yet, when I went in before supper, I could have sworn that it was properly made.

'You haven't been lying down, have you?' Chard asked.

'You know I haven't. I've been with you all the while.'

'But before supper'

'Before supper I wasn't in here more than a minute. I certainly didn't touch the bed, and I am willing to swear that it wasn't like this.'

'And since then,' said Chard musingly, 'we've been having supper in the next room and sitting outside this very window. Yes, Yoxall's quite right. Queer things happen here if this is a sample.'

I drew back the bedclothes. There was a slight indentation of the mattress, visible on the sheet that covered it, the print of a human body.

I wondered why it was so plainly visible until I touched it; then I drew back with a sharp cry.

'It's all wet!' I exclaimed. 'Somebody wet through has been lying on my bed!'

The pillow was deeply dented, as if by a head, and it was wringing wet.

As I picked it up to show it to Chard, I caught another whiff of that foul, stale river smell.

'H'm!' he said. 'It looks as if we shall have to spend another night here.'

'Why?' I asked. I had been frightened before, but to be frank I liked the present occasion less than any of my previous adventures with Chard.

'Because,' he said, 'I think that whatever happens here of a night has happened already, and we've missed it. I'll have this room tomorrow night. Or perhaps mine gets a turn. It's impossible to say.'

I had already thought of sleeping elsewhere, but I took heart of grace through Chard's opinion that the manifestations were over for the night.

There were more bedclothes in the linen cupboard, and I laid a ground-sheet over the mattress. It was comforting to know that only a thin partition separated Chard's room from mine.

'We can call out for each other if necessary,' he said; arid indeed, while we undressed we were able to carry on a conversation without raising our voices.

When I had blown out my candle and got into bed I found the high moon looking straight on me through the open French window. I have never enjoyed sleeping with my face in moonlight, but to shield myself I must have drawn the blind. I needed all the air I could get to guard against a return of that foul river smell, so I chose the lesser of two evils, knowing that the moon would soon pass.

It vanished after a few minutes, but its light still flooded the garden and flung a pale ivory flag on the wall behind my head. I lay with my face turned to the window, listening to the unceasing and unchanging roar of the weir, and the lisp and lap of water about the landing-stage. For a long while I could not sleep, but I must have dozed at last, for I woke suddenly in cold horror, still staring at the open window.

The long open window now framed the figure of a woman. The moonlight played full upon her, but she seemed to diffuse a light of her own—a stale, dingy phosphorescence. She wore a pale green cotton dress which, being sodden, clung to her figure like a glove. She was horribly bloated, and her hair, smooth and wet on the crown of her head, hung about her shoulders in bedraggled tangles. It was impossible to guess if she were old or young, for her face was puffed out, and a muddy-grey in colour. It was the face of somebody who had been in the water for some considerable time. But she was still able to control the muscles of that dreadful unhuman countenance. An eye, dead and bloodshot, rolled on me in a dreadful travesty of coquetry; the swollen lips leered invitation. I saw, in a moment of unutterable horror, that her hair was matted with mud and laced with river weed.

Next moment she had stepped into the room. She had lost a shoe and a naked foot protruded from a few rags of stocking, but in the other shoe I heard the squelch of water as she moved.

For some ghastly, unspeakable period of time I had lost the nerves of motion. They returned as suddenly as they left me. I found myself suddenly out of bed upon the other side, and rushing for the door, while my own shriek echoed in my ears. It woke Chard, for he was already out of bed when I rushed into his room.

I must have told him something coherent. I can remember stammering out something in my terror. He lit a candle and left me, and I dropped on my knees beside his bed and buried my face in the clothes. But he was back in half a minute, white to the lips.

'Yes,' he said unsteadily, 'she's in there. I think we'll go and sleep out in the punt—if we're to get any sleep at all.'

I am not a coward, but I had to brace myself before re-entering in my room in the broad sunlight of the following morning, and while I was there I felt qualms of disgust which amounted to nausea.

Chard was still shaken, but perfectly calm and collected.

'Yes,' he said, 'she was evidently drowned. And every night she comes back out of the water to look for somebody '

'To look for Rushby,' I said quickly.

'Yes,' said Chard, 'perhaps Rushby. But we can begin to make inquiries now. We have had our—er—experiences. '

'If I thought I was ever likely to have such another,' I said grimly, 'you'd have to find a new companion, Chard. '

Our charwoman arrived at eight o'clock, and Chard called her into the sitting-room.

'We want to talk to you,' he said gently. 'Did you work for Mr Rushby when he was here?'

She lowered her gaze and seemed confused.

'Yes, sir. I worked for him,' she said at last, almost with an air of confession.

'Do you happen to know why he sold the bungalow?'

'Yes, sir. I thought everybody knew that. Everybody about here, that is.'

'Then do you mind telling us all about it, please?'

'There's no harm in me tellin' you, since everybody knows. It was along of a scandal. He'll never dare show his face on this reach of the river again. He was always all right to me, mind you. I worked for him, and I knew what went on. It wasn't any business of mine, and if I'd made it my business I shouldn't have got any work at all. He used to have young ladies—or rather young women—down here. There's plenty of that, and worse, goin' on all around. This is a wicked place. I wonder it hasn't been wiped out before now, like them cities in the Bible.

'One weekend last year, he brought down a girl—a chorus girl she turned out to be afterwards, who was out of work for the time being. It was early in the season, just after the spring floods, and the water was high and the current running strong. 'T wasn't too safe on the river for people as didn't understand what they was doin', but on the Sunday he must needs take 'er out and learn her the punt.

'You can guess what happened. She went overboard, and he didn't seem to make no effort to save her. Lost his head completely, it seems. The body was carried miles downstream, and it was a week before they found her. And when the inquest came on the coroner gave Mr Rushby a nice choking-off for havin' done nothing and just let her drown.

'Mr Rushby left suddenly after that, for a lot of young gentlemen about here were calling him a coward and threatenin' to throw him in the river if he dared show his face anywhere about. I'm sorry for him in a way, because p'raps he couldn't swim very well, and nobody knows what they're goin' to do once they've lost their 'ead. But I'm sorrier still for the girl. She couldn't have been fit to die, poor thing!'

And there the story ends. I don't know what became of that good sport, Mr Rushby, but I am sure I know why he sold his bungalow.

'Munki Puz' is once more a bower of roses this summer. It is as charming as ever in the daytime, and I daresay as terrible as ever after dusk.

It still belongs to Yoxall, but he never uses it. He is too honest to dispose of it, as it was sold to him, but anyone knowing what he is prepared to tell them may buy it as it stands for a purely nominal sum.

The Protector

It was towards the end of July, and Chard and I were making plans to go westward for golf and fishing when Gervase Langtree's letter arrived. It was written on notepaper headed 'Rowans House, Medleigh College, Dorset', and it briefly asked for an interview on the following day.

'Housemaster, I should think,' said Chard, tossing me the letter. 'Pass me Paton, will you?'

I reached for the book and then read the letter while Chard found what he sought.

'Yes,' he said presently, 'here we are. There seems to be fourteen housemasters at Medleigh, and here's Mr G.L.G. Langtree (M.A., Oxon), number six on the list. Wonder what he wants. Well, if it's anything down in Dorset we can oblige him without much trouble to ourselves. It'll be on our way.'

Everybody knows Medleigh, which is now recognised as one of the best of the second-class public schools. It is an old foundation, but it had remained a humble country grammar-school until the middle of last century, when a famous headmaster had raised its status, and incidentally its fees, and had succeeded in multiplying its numbers by nearly ten.

'I never heard of a haunted school before,' I remarked.

'Oh, didn't you?' Chard laughed. 'We were supposed to have a ghost or two at my old place.'

'So were we for that matter,' I said, 'but nobody ever saw them.'

Chard considered.

'All the schools,' he remarked, 'have just closed down for the summer holidays. Well, after all, it may not be at Medleigh that our services are required. I think I'll ring up this Mr Langtree and ask him. If he wants to see us down there we can save him a journey to town by taking it in our stride, so to speak. Oh, good! He's got his telephone number on the notepaper, I see.'

Chard put a call through at once, and, not unexpectedly, was kept waiting three-quarters of an hour before being summoned to the telephone outside.

After three or four minutes he returned.

'Well,' he said, 'I got through, and I've been talking to our friend Langtree. We couldn't hear each other very well. But he seemed to want me to come to Medleigh, and he gladly extended the invitation to you. So I said we'd be with him some time tomorrow afternoon or evening.'

Medleigh is not on one of the great main roads, and neither Chard nor I had so much as passed through it before. We found it to be a funny little old-world town of about seven thousand inhabitants, dominated by the school. This stood at the far end of the town, and consisted of a number of large and almost modem buildings grouped around the original Elizabethan structure, which now formed the base of a long and deep quadrangle. As we passed on we saw, through gaps in the buildings, the long, level playing-fields behind, stretching away into the distance. Some of the houses were detached and even distant, and Rowans House must have been some five hundred yards west of the main block.

A young butler admitted us and conducted us into a light, well-furnished drawing-room, and within a minute the door had opened once more and Mr Langtree had entered.

He was a tall, lean man of fifty-something, with grey hair and moustache, and he wore the undefinable stamp of the schoolmaster. His accent was unaffectedly 'Oxford', and he gave the impression of being narrow and genial and well-meaning, and perpetually harassed. He thanked us effusively for coming, begged us to sit down, and said that he had ordered tea, all in one long unpunctuated sentence.

'I've just packed my wife and family off to Jersey,' he said, by way of beginning a more consecutive conversation, 'whither I propose to follow them in a few days. But if you can stay tonight, or longer, as I trust you intend doing, I think I can make you comfortable. The boys' quarters are upside down at the moment—being thoroughly cleaned out, you understand—but their part of the house is shut off entirely from mine. Forty of them went off three days ago, and the place seems empty. Peace, perfect peace!' And he laughed.

Tea, thin bread and butter and cake arrived, and we sat around a little table gleaming with silver. My cup was already empty for the first time when Chard suddenly said, 'Now, Mr Langtree, I think you know very well what we are waiting for you to tell us.'

He uttered a little, self-conscious, neighing laugh.

'At least,' he said, 'I needn't feel embarrassed in the presence of you gentlemen for believing in something which I am now compelled to believe I must confess that until the end of last term—no, I mean the spring term—I had been a complete Sadducee as regards—er—ghosts. And now the affair is becoming serious. You know what a school is, Mr Chard, and what parents are. I know for a fact that some boys are begging to be taken away. We have a long waiting-list, it is true, but one doesn't want stories to get around, and one doesn't want a houseful of boys with nerves. The headmaster pooh-poohs the whole affair. Indeed, I daren't confess to him that I have good reason for sharing the prevalent belief. He came down to the House one evening about a month ago and lectured the boys on the folly and wickedness of superstition. I think you know, Mr Chard, that the average healthy English boy is not superstitious.'

Chard nodded and smiled.

'I think we understand all your difficulties, Mr Langtree,' he said. 'If you will kindly tell us as concisely and consecutively as you can what has been troubling you we will do our best to help you. '

Langtree poured out more tea for us.

'At the end of last February,' he began, 'a tragedy happened here. I had better begin by telling you that we play out-matches at Rugger in the autumn term, and play off the house matches in the first two months of the spring term. And in a house match last February one of my boys, named Grimshaw, died on the field.

'It was nobody's fault. Grimshaw was apparently a normally healthy boy of sixteen and a-half, and he had played in the third fifteen pack all the preceding terms. Apparently, from what the post-mortem revealed, he must have been an unconscious sufferer from indigestion and from some unsuspected weakness of the heart. He simply collapsed suddenly and died. 'Fortunately perhaps for me—it may sound callous, but still I say it—he had no near relatives. He had a guardian who performed his duties in a perfunctory manner and seldom saw the boy. Grimshaw used to spend his holidays with different masters or under the care of holiday tutors. We were all tremendously sorry for the boy, but—well, one was humanly glad that he hadn't parents who would perhaps naturally accuse us here of gross negligence.

'Of course, his death was a profound shock to the whole school. He wasn't exactly a popular boy—not popular as one generally understands the word—but nobody disliked him, and everybody seemed to respect him. He had a curious kind of dignity of his own. Even when he was a much smaller boy the big boys used to speak to him civilly, and I never heard of any crowd of youngsters trying to rag him. Of course, the staff liked him because he worked hard and gave no trouble. I had intended making him a prefect as soon as he got into the Sixth.

'And now I must explain that upstairs there is a large schoolroom in which the House assembles for morning and evening prayers, and in which the smaller boys do their preparation. At the end of the room there is a blackboard and chalk, so that any boy needing help may be given a hasty demonstration. Next door is the house library, and the two librarians—both boys, of course—are given ten minutes' grace after night prayers to tidy up.

That is to say, they Eire supposed to put away any books which may be lying about, fold up the papers, and put the magazines back on the middle table. And it is also their duty to see that the blackboard in the next room is left clean.

'Well, about a week after Grimshaw's funeral I came down as usual to read prayers, and saw nearly every' pair of eyes focused on the blackboard. I turned to see what they were looking at, and just to the left of the middle of the blackboard was chalked the word "Be". It began boldly enough, but grew faint towards the end of the second and last letter. The unpleasant thing about it was that it seemed an unmistakable imitation of poor Grimshaw's handwriting. I must tell you that he made all his letters squat and broad, and his capital B's had a thick loop as this one had.

'I snatched up a duster then and there, and wiped it out. I must own that I was furious and upset, having little doubt that some oaf had purposely imitated the dead boy's handwriting. The inanity and the grossly bad taste of the joke appalled me. But I made no comment to the boys. They are gentlemen, and I knew that they felt as I felt. The culprit, if he were discovered, could safely be left to my two prefects, or, for that matter, to the rank and file. But I afterwards casually inquired of the librarians if they had cleaned the blackboard over-night, and they assured me that they had.

'Next morning the blackboard was placed a little nearer the front row of desks, and a succession of boys coming into the room rubbed it with their shoulders, until one—probably on purpose—knocked it off its easel. I came into the room just as it was being picked up. There was a little smudge in the middle as if something had been rubbed off, but it was a very small smudge, and it was then impossible to distinguish what mark had originally been there.

'Next day I came into the room to find another imitation—as I naturally thought—of poor Grimshaw's handwriting. And this time it was another part of the verb to be. The words "Are", all in small letters, was scribbled across the middle, and once more the final "e" was faint and thin. I could read in the boys' faces just what I felt myself. Some young fool was practising a kind of caddish humour which we don't encourage here.

'Again I questioned the two librarians. They both assured me that they had cleaned the blackboard before going to bed, and that Jarvis, one of the servants, had waited outside to lock up the room. The affair was even more inexplicable because Jarvis had unlocked the room again in the morning, and remembered seeing the word there as he passed through. I may add that the two boys who acted as librarians were entirely above suspicion.

'After that we had no more of that sort of writing on the blackboard, but it proved to be only the beginning of a series of extraordinary happenings. About a week later Venner, my head prefect, came to me and said there was something he ought to report Young Keene had been going about the house saying that he had seen a ghost, and before Venner could tell me I guessed whose ghost it was.

'Venner's point of view was simple. A boy who saw a ghost ought afterwards to see a doctor. Having assured himself that young Keene was not rotting—and only a rotter would rot about poor Grimshaw—he had come to me with the unspoken suggestion that Keene had gone off his head. The queer thing was, he said, that Keene didn't seem frightened or nervous. He was just solemn about it all.

'So I interviewed Keene and extracted from him the coy confession that he had gone downstairs in the dead of night to get cigarettes from his locker in the dayroom, so that he could smoke out of the dormitory window. And in the dayroom he had come face to face with Grimshaw, who had smiled and tried to speak. Grimshaw', he said, was wearing his football things—his black-and-white House jersey—just as when he died. "It's no use telling me I imagined it, sir," he said to me. "I just know I didn't. And the queer thing was that I wasn't in the least afraid. I think he tried to say something, because his lips moved, although he couldn't speak. And then he melted into a sort of mist, which faded away while I stood looking at it."

'Well, what could I do? I could only tell the boy not to be foolish, and not to talk about his hallucination to the other boys. I gathered afterwards that he was mildly ragged, and then the affair began to be forgotten—until Grimshaw was seen by two other boys on successive nights.

'They too were not in the least alarmed. They were awed and calm and very serious. But the rest of the house began to get very nervy, and the Easter holidays came as a relief.

'This last term the—er—the wraith of Grimshaw has been seen on four different occasions. In the summer term the bigger boys studying for examinations are allowed to sit up late, and one morning in May a boy of seventeen named Tomlinson asked for an interview with me. He looked shaken and upset. He said that on his way to bed at about eleven o'clock on the previous night he had looked out of the window and seen a hideous and disgusting-looking monster—something like a homed toad, he said, but the size of a man—slinking into the shrubbery. It looked as if it were cowering away from something, and as he watched in horror, Grimshaw came into view under the window. "I haven't said a word to anybody about it," he said, "but I thought I ought to tell you, sir."

'Of course I had to tell him he'd been dreaming—the thing still seemed incredible to me—and beg him to pursue his policy of silence. But about a fortnight later, when the eleven came back very late after the Rampley match, and Venner, whom I trusted most implicitly, told me that he had distinctly seen Grimshaw on the stairs, my incredulity received a very serious shock. And then—about a fortnight ago—I saw Grimshaw myself.

'I was in my study late one night answering letters, when something made me look up. He was standing by the door. It was Grimshaw unmistakably, just as I had last seen him alive. I think I can honestly say that I wasn't afraid, but I felt awed, and I was intensely interested. I sprang up and asked him what he wanted. He smiled shyly at me and tried to speak, but I didn't hear a sound. And then he faded away like breath from a mirror, and left me standing there staring at nothing. So you see, Mr Chard, I too must believe. And now that I believe I must act. Mr Chard, can you tell me what I ought to do?'

Chard was silent for a full minute.

'You want these visitations to cease?' he said at last.

'Of course! Of course! Half the boys who haven't seen him have been terrified. I have seen stark fear in their eyes. But if the poor fellow has some message to convey, I should like to hear it. Something is troubling his poor spirit, Mr Chard. '

Chard nodded.

'I will see what I can do,' he said. 'By the way, apart from the newusness of the boys, have you had a pretty clean bill of health here lately?'

'It has been wonderful,' said Langtree, waxing suddenly enthusiastic.

'Last term was a record. Indeed, ever since poor Grimshaw died I don't think we have had a single boy on the sick list. And now, if you don't mind, I'll show you over the house.'

Chard and I were left alone a little later. He turned to me suddenly with a smile and said, 'This is really an extraordinarily interesting case. What do you think of the homed toad about the size of a man which Grimshaw was seen driving away from the house?'

'Only one boy saw that,' I answered non-committally.

'H'm! Do you happen to know what an elemental is?'

'Isn't it some sort of malevolent spirit which never had a body?'

'I should probably answer that question with the same beautiful vagueness. But I suppose you know that in certain savage countries diseases are supposed to be devils—that is, elementals—and the witch-doctor is sent for to cast the devil out of the patient. There may be a lot to be said for that point of view, you know. '

He paused and smiled.

'The dead boy,' he continued, 'had no home and no people, and all his devotion was probably centred on the school, and particularly on this house. Now why did he write on the blackboard merely parts of an auxiliary verb—"Be" and "Are"? There's not much sense in that, is there? It savours of those childish messages which are rapped out on tables and written by the planchette, words and fragments of words without meaning.'

'Just what I've been thinking,' I remarked.

'Well,' said Chard suavely, 'you've been thinking wrong. His materialised spirit hadn't the strength to write more than a letter or two at a time. It took him three evenings to write one short word. You will remember that after he had written "B-E" and before he had written "A-R-E" something was rubbed out. And unless I'm altogether out in my calculations, that something was the letter "W". Now what does "B-E-W-A-R-E" spell?'

I stared at Chard and smiled.

'That's ingenious!' I exclaimed.

'On the contrary, it's simple. Some danger has been threatening the boys, and this young spirit has been keeping it at bay. When it passes he too may pass. But we may know more about that tonight. We will sit 111 that room where the blackboard is, and see if he will come to us.'

We took leave of our host shortly after eleven o'clock and went up to the bare, severe, desk-lined room next to the library, and we sat down side by side at two desks on which generations of boys had carved names and initials. It was not dark. The moon looked at us through a high window on our left hand, and we could read the date on the calendar overhanging the high rostrum at the far end of the room. Strangely enough, I did not feel in the least nervous. I was eager and expectant, and mingled with it all was a kind of pity. My surroundings brought into my heart a queer echo of sentiment. I defy any man to sit quietly in a schoolroom without being taken back to his own youth.

Presently Chard began to speak. His voice rose scarcely above a whisper, and he was not speaking to me.

'Grimshaw,' he called softly, 'come to us, won't you? We understand, and we want to help you. Give your message to us, and we will pass it on. Show yourself to us, Grimshaw. We only want to help you.'

He spoke in the wheedling tone of one who addresses a child or a sick patient, a tone which implored confidence. I looked over my shoulder to see if anything lurked in the shadows behind me, and when I turned my gaze once more to look straight ahead the boy was there.

He stood at the top of the passage between the double row of desks, a pathetic figure still in the mud-stained uniform of football. He was looking straight at Chard with a smile which was very shy, very boyish and very young. I don't think I was at all scared of him. I was conscious of pity and awe and reverence, but not of fear. Chard sat quite still and went on speaking.

'What's the matter, old chap?' he asked quietly. 'Can we help you? You want to tell Mr Langtree something? Isn't that it?'

There was a quick nod, and the face lit up with eagerness. The lips moved.

'We can't hear you,' said Chard gently. 'Can you write it?'

The boyish figure turned at once to the blackboard. A few stubs of chalk lay on the ledge. I saw the boy struggle to lift one. It was as if he were trying to raise some load which weighed hundredweights. He dropped it at last and turned to look at Chard with a deprecatory smile.

'Never mind,' Chard said, in the same quiet reverberating voice. 'I think I can help you without that. I will ask you some questions, and you shall nod or shake your head. You don't like being here? You've a happier place to go to, haven't you, old chap?'

The head drooped a little in answer.

'You're here for a purpose, then?'

The head drooped again.

'Some danger threatening the boys?'

Again the answer was 'Yes'.

'And you're warding it off?'

The same answer.

'Is it some kind of illness?'

Again there was the same motion of the head.

'I see. And when the danger is over you'll go away and be happy somewhere else? Is that it?'

The spirit face smiled and wore a look of ineffable relief.

'Ah,' said Chard softly, 'I thought I was right. I'll tell Mr Langtree, and he will understand. Everybody will be very grateful to you, Grimshaw. You will do your duty to the house while there is need, and afterwards you will be very happy and peaceful—very happy and very peaceful, won't you, Grimshaw?'

Again the head inclined and the face brightened with its growing smile. I was conscious of the smile even after he had gone. We did not see him go, but Chard and I were suddenly alone.

Ten minutes later we were talking to Langtree in his study.

'That faithful spirit,' said Chard, 'is standing between your house and one of the Powers of Darkness. There is danger threatening, and when the danger is past he will not be seen again.'

Early in the autumn Chard came to see me with a folded newspaper in his hand.

'Have you read this about Medleigh School?' he asked. 'It's shut up for the rest of the term. There's been a sudden outbreak of cerebro-spinal meningitis. Every house has been affected except one. Knowing what you know, perhaps you can guess the name of the house that escaped.'

'Rowans?' I said immediately.

'Yes,' said Chard, 'Rowans. Here's the report.'

The Girl in Blue

I had been associated with Francis Chard for some years before he told me the story which I am about to re-tell. When I first met him he was already a profound student of occultism, and afterwards, when I once asked him what had first turned his steps in that direction, he smiled and said,

'Curiosity, I suppose, and a love of the mysterious, and a natural bent that way.'

It was not until recently that I learned the tale of his first 'experience'.

We were travelling back from Devonshire by the night train after one of our many disappointments. The haunted house, which we had just visited by invitation, had been—at least, during our stay—barren of phenomena. Yet our host and hostess had a wealth of uncanny stories to tell us about their place of abode, and seemed genuinely distressed when at last we had to leave them, without having shared any of their experiences or having been able to suggest any explanation or remedy.

We had already tired of reading while the train was rushing through Somerset, and laid aside our evening papers almost at the same instant. I leaned over towards Chard, seeing that he was not in the least disposed to doze.

'What do you make of the Cherretts and Homdown House?' I asked.

'They struck me as being quite honest and truthful people.'

'So they did me,' Chard confessed. 'I think probably they had some cause to feel disturbed. But all that kind of phenomena isn't objective. They may be able to see and hear what we couldn't see and hear.'

'But if their ghost were subjective, surely you are sufficiently—what's the beastly word?— "psychic", to be sensitive of its presence?'

Chard shook his head.

'I never pretended to be sensitive,' he said, 'and I am not sure that anybody really is. That's a word which cuts a lot of ice with imaginative old ladies, who always remember ghostly dreams and warnings shortly after the dire event has happened. But I hold it possible in certain cases for a man or a woman to see and hear things which nobody else can see and hear. And in nine cases out of ten they and their friends put it down to imagination.'

'And that,' I said, 'is after all the most reasonable solution.'

'Not if some other factor intervenes. I know a case of a boy at a public school who passed his house-master's son on the stairs one evening. On entering his house-master's study a little later he said, "Oh, sir, I see Dick's come home." This Dick, by the way, had been in Jamaica for the past two years. The boy was told that he must have been dreaming. Yet it transpired shortly afterwards that Dick had been killed some thousands of miles away at the very time when he had been seen by his old schoolfellow. Nobody saw Dick but this one boy, but to say that it was imagination on his part is to credit a coincidence far more extraordinary than the wildest tales of ghostly apparitions. Besides, there was my own experience.'

'Which one?'

'The one that converted me. Haven't I told you? I was quite an unsympathetic sceptic until I was twenty-three. But I was still more sceptical about the powers of my imagination and any tricks my subconscious mind might be able to play on my ulterior consciousness. I never had "imagined things", and I don't believe other people imagine things on the grand scale which is airily taken for granted. When something happened to me I realised that it had actually happened. Besides, I learned something afterwards which put the matter beyond all reasonable doubt.'

'You never told me the story,' I said. 'I often wondered what was your first experience.'

'I'll tell you now, if you like,' Chard replied. 'It affected me so much that I am not likely to make many mistakes about details, even at this distance of time. Come and sit over here next to me, so that I needn't shout. O, Lord, we're only going through Taunton now. I've got half the night to tell you.'

'You know,' Chard began, 'that I started life as a journalist, hoping to make enough that way to let me read for the Bar. I'd passed one law exam at Oxford, but my father, a poor Warwickshire parson, had spent all his savings on my education, and I couldn't continue to take an allowance from him after I came down.

'I had, I suppose, just about an average mental equipment for wresting a livelihood out of Fleet Street. I'd contributed one or two things to Isis, which I fondly believed contained the germ of genius, and published, at my own expense, a slim volume of verse.

'I soon found that 'Varsity men were not particularly appreciated on the Street. The kind of reporter most in request was the sort of youth who was ready and willing to kick open the bedroom door of a dying duchess in order to learn from her own lips the tale of some youthful indiscretion. There were, of course, little cliques of self-styled highbrows, who irritated me exceedingly and who contributed for nothing, or next to nothing, to pretentious little reviews which were subsidised by literary patrons with more money than sense. Well, I couldn't afford their company, and I couldn't afford to be a litterateur, so I took two rooms down in Chelsea and approached Fleet Street by the back door.

'I didn't do so badly by free-lancing. It was hard work, but I didn't mind that, and I made a living. I was able to turn my hand to most things, and among other jobs I did a bit of football reporting on the strength of having just missed my Rugger Blue. This nearly cost me my life, for I went out on a foul day with a feverish cold to the Blackheath-Harlequins match, and the next I knew I was on my back with pleurisy and pneumonia.

'My two rooms were in a house on one of those mean streets in Chelsea between King's Road and the Embankment. My landlady's name I shall never forget, for it was Cluttonhole. I saw little of her, because I was seldom in, save when I had work to do at night. I took all my meals out except breakfast, for there was an excellent and cheap little restaurant within three minutes' walk, and the exigencies of my work often kept me far away during the day.

'Mrs Cluttonhole inhabited a dungeon-like basement, into which I had not ventured before my illness. She was a shrivelled little woman with an appalling cast in one eye, and in spite of many unfortunate financial experiences with a long succession of lodgers she still maintained a high regard for those whom she was pleased to call Bohemian gents.

'Her ground floor was let to a man and his wife, whom I saw no more than twice during my stay. The man went out every evening, and did not return until breakfast time, which argues that he was either on the night staff of a paper or else a professional burglar. I had the next floor all to myself, or rather I shared it with the one bathroom of the establishment, which was necessarily public property. There was another floor above mine—possibly two. I gathered by the sounds of voices, mostly female, that the rooms above me were never tenantless for long, although it was seldom that I caught so much as a fleeting glimpse of one of their occupants.

'I didn't send for a doctor until I had to, and then I was hors de combat. He would have had me moved if it had been possible, and as it wasn't possible he sent for a nurse. He also wrote to my father, who came and stayed next door—the house I was in being full—until I had passed the crisis.

'Like all good patients I hated my nurse during my periods of consciousness in the early stages of my illness. She was one of those professional, pillow-shaking, dictatorial women who seem to think that the best way to save a patient is to make him uncomfortable. Of course, I was delirious a lot of the time, and I hope I told her some home-truths. My wallpaper was a chaste design of red roses in blue baskets, and red birds sitting on blue birds' nests. Many a time I saw those birds flying round and round the room as if somebody had fired a gun inside an aviary.

'After a while I became aware that my nurse had an assistant, whom I liked almost as much as I disliked the nurse herself. She was a pretty, fair-haired girl in a long, pale blue dress— they wore dresses long in those days—and there was something about her which seemed to my sick fancy intensely lovable. I noticed even in my semi-conscious state that she had a perfect figure like a nymph's, willowy without being thin, which bore her head as gracefully as a stalk bears a flower.

'Sometimes she was in the room with the nurse, who seemed strangely unaware of her presence. Only when I grew rebellious at some necessary attention on the nurse's part she would shake her head and smile at me half roguishly, as if to say, "Now, you must be a good boy and put up with all this if you want to get better."

'Often, when the nurse was out of the room, she would peep inside and smile at me, and then sometimes she would come gently across the room and shake up my pillows, smiling very sweetly at me all the while. The odd thing was, I thought, that she never spoke.

'Sometimes I addressed her in the nurse's presence, but she lingered in the background, and the nurse used to give the least hitch to her shoulders—an indication, I thought, of professional jealousy. On one occasion when I found myself about to endure having my head raised and my pillow punched by the hands of the professional I called out peevishly,

"Oh, I don't want you! If it's got to be done, let her do it."

' "Let who do it?" demanded the nurse.

' "The nice girl in blue."

' "Oh, her," said the nurse shortly, and proceeded to do it herself. But I was fortified by a humorous shake of the head and a roguish smile from the other side of the room.

'One afternoon I heard the doctor talking to my father outside the door. I was getting along very nicely now, I was glad to hear. But was I engaged to be married, or were—er—my affections in any way engaged? Because, if so it might be as well to get the young lady to come and see me.

'My father replied that he did not know of such lady.

' "Well," said the doctor, "who's the girl in blue he's always talking about?"

'I chuckled to myself. If the doctor didn't understand that it was the girl who came in to help nurse me he was a bigger idiot than I'd taken him for.

'Time wore on, and as the birds on the wallpaper took flight less frequently, and absurd and tangled threads of problems wore my mind less and less often, so the visits of the girl in blue became fewer and fewer. They ceased altogether about a week before the nurse went away. I often inquired after her, and received always an evasive reply. This I thought was because the nurse was annoyed at my preferring the ministrations of somebody else.

' "Now that I've turned the comer," I thought, "she's left me alone. The only thing to do is to get better as soon as possible, find out who she is, and thank her."

'Oh, but I got far beyond thanking her in my dreams! I was twenty-three, and it wasn't hard for me to persuade myself that I loved her, and that she was the one girl whom it would be possible for me to marry. The thought made me restless and happy by turns, but at least it kept my mind occupied and helped me rapidly to mend.

'My father could not afford the time to stay near me after I was out of danger, and I could not afford to retain the services of the nurse a day after it was possible to dispense with them. So, while I was still confined to bed and three parts helpless I found myself suddenly left alone.

'Mrs Cluttonhole was a brick. I had only to tug at the bell-rope which hung down beside the bed to bring her up from the basement. She waited on me hand and foot, and sometimes came and sat with me. But she had plenty to do without having a sick man on her hands, and I was alone for twenty-two hours out of the twenty-four.

'It was then that I began to appreciate my loneliness and helplessness. Even after these years I remember every feature of the room, every picture, and every crack in the ceiling. My bed was a double one, and faced the one window, which was kept open at the top. The upper sash used to annoy me for being slightly aslant when the window was open, and even when the holland blind was down I could see behind it a crooked bar of shadow. There were three pictures, none of which was artistically satisfying, and all reproductions. One depicted an Eastern lady balancing a pitcher on her head and walking on a tiled floor; another was entitled "I'se nearly as big as you, Doggie", which speaks for itself; and the third represented a gentleman of the early nineteenth century in the act of not being on speaking terms with a lady of the same period at the other end of a rustic seat. What they had found to quarrel about was not clear, unless one or other had spoken disrespectfully of the sundial which occupied the foreground.

'The door was on the left of the bed. On the right was the fireplace. Between the fireplace and the end of the wall was an enormous mahogany wardrobe, of which the mirror focussed the sun for about five minutes every morning. I soon learned to know the time when I saw a splash of light on the opposite wall. I won't bore you with any more details, although they are all photographed on my mind, but I got to know that room as a prisoner knows his cell. Only loneliness can do that for a man, and I was lonelier than I had ever been before or have been since. Now that my father had returned home I had no friends in London—at least, none who knew both my plight and my address.

'I began to regret even the absence of the nurse, and Mrs Cluttonhole's visits were rays of sunshine. I lost no time in inquiring of her about the girl in blue, and she rolled an arch swivel eye on me.

' "Oh," she said, "you mean Miss Smith, what used to be upstairs?"

' "I mean the girl who used to come in and see me when I was really bad."

' "That was Miss Smith. Top floor back."

' "Why doesn't she come and see me now?"

' "Because she've lef."

' "Left!"

' "She bein' on the stage and havin' got a job."

'I knew how my face had fallen.

' "Will she be coming back here?" I asked.

' "Of course, she will. Let me think now. They're at 'Uddersfield next week, Leeds week after—let me see, in about a month they'll be at the King's, 'Ammersmith, and she's bound to come and stop with me for that week."

'I was only partly comforted. I wanted to see her soon, and desperately. Strangely enough I couldn't bring myself to think of her as Miss Smith. Somehow the name didn't fit her. I just thought of her as the Blue Girl.

'I remember that that was one of the nights when I couldn't sleep. I had already started smoking again, against the advice of my doctor, and coming in to see me before retiring for the night Mrs Cluttonhole had placed my cigarettes and matches out of the way of easy temptation, or, in other words, on the wash-stand. She had also drawn my blind over the length of the open window, because it had come on to drizzle.

'Try as I would I could not sleep. I turned in every direction, and twisted into every posture, exploring every comer of the bed for coolness. It would have comforted me to smoke, but my condition of lassitude left me too infirm of purpose to get out of bed and toil across the room for my cigarettes. It had stopped raining now, and the moon was up, and I longed for the blind to be raised and to taste the sweet, unfiltered air from outside.

'In the faint light there was nothing on which to rest the eyes. I had not even the doubtful joys of tracing the cracks in the ceiling and likening them to the rivers and lakes of some great unexplored land. Every quarter of an hour brought a chorus from the London clocks, and my quest of sleep became more desperate, and therefore more hopeless. An intense depression overtook me, and I called out after the weak and pitiable fashion of a sick man, "Blue Girl! Oh, come to me! Come to me!"

'I have said that I cried out, but I could have spoken scarcely above a whisper. Yet it was as if she had been waiting outside for sound of my voice. The door opened, and there she stood under the lintel smiling at me, before she took a further step into the room and turned to close it. It was that smile which had always soothed me, and there was kindness and healing in her eyes.

'She seemed to know just what I wanted without my telling her. She went straight to the window and the blind ran up with a clatter, letting in the moonlight upon her fair hair. Then she went to the wash-stand, and I heard the rattle of matches. She brought them, and the yellow packet of cigarettes, over to the chair on the right of my bed. I thanked her, although quite briefly, for I wanted to ask her questions.

' "Where have you been all this time, Blue Girl?"

'She shook her head, and her smile became enigmatical.

' "Speak to me. Why do you never speak?"

'Once more the shake of the head, only this time it was accompanied by a look which said plainly, "You must not talk to me now. You must get to sleep as soon as you can, or I shan't come to see you again."

'She shook the pillow behind my head, and I was aware of the touch of a cool hand on my hair. I seemed to have lost all resolution, bathed as I suddenly was in an atmosphere of love and comfort. Then she gave me a smile like a caress and went. I smoked half a cigarette, and then I felt myself dozing, so I pinched it out and fell asleep.

'When I woke up next morning I am bound to confess that I lay still for some minutes, wondering if I had dreamed it all. Looking back, there was something dream-like in the experience. Then I roused myself a little and looked around me. There on the chair beside my bed were the matches and the cigarette packet, with my half-smoked cigarette lying on top. And the window-blind was raised as high as it would go.

'Presently Mrs Cluttonhole came in and proceeded to scold me after the arch fashion peculiar to her kind.

' "Bad, wicked Mr Chard! After I made you comfortable for the night you risks your life by gettin' out of bed for your cigarettes, and pulls your blind up."

' "I didn't," I said triumphantly. "And you were wrong about the Blue Girl. She's still in the house, and you must have been thinking of someone else. It was she who came and raised my blind and brought me my cigarettes."

'Mrs Cluttonhole stared at me rather angrily.

' "If I hear any more about any Blue Girls," she said, "I'll get the doctor to you again. The idea! And don't you go gettin' out of bed at night when you ain't got the strength."

'I couldn't then conceive why Mrs Cluttonhole should display indignation at my mentioning the Blue Girl. She was the last kind of woman, and too genuine a piece of Old Chelsea, for her sense of proprieties to be offended. Moreover, I could not understand why she had stalled me off with a story about the girl being an actress away on tour. By a coincidence the doctor, who called less often now', put in an appearance later on in the morning, and took my temperature and asked if I had felt any symptoms of fever.

'I did not see her the following night or the night after. But on my next sleepless night she was with me like a ministering angel. I saw her perhaps half-a-dozen more times, until the night arrived when I had permission actually to get up and dress for a few hours on the day following.

'I was thinking of her when she came, and for the first time I remarked a hint of sadness in her smile. Her soothing hands once more kneaded the pillow behind my head.
' "Thank you, Blue Girl," I said. And then, looking up into her eyes, I added, "Blue Girl, I do love you so!"

'Instantly she bent swiftly and kissed me. I felt her lips warm on my brow. My hands were buried under the clothes, and before I could uncover them and hold them out to her she was gone beyond arm's reach. It was a gesture of farewell on her part, but I, although I read it correctly, was not distressed. She must have heard, I thought, that tomorrow was to begin my convalescence, and that I should need her no more. But I knew that she was living in the house, and I told myself that all I had to do was to seek her out. From the door she gave me one last, unforgettable look. Then she went. 'I hadn't been up an hour next day when I had a surprise visitor. My friend Simpson, late of B N.C., came bounding into my sitting-room.

' "Hullo, young fellow!" he said, "I've just been hearing about you. Why didn't you let me know before? I've a closed car outside, and you're coming down to my place at Brighton for a month. Now go and find your toothbrush, and don't argue."

'I didn't argue much. Tire offer was too good to be missed. But I didn't stay a month. I came back to all intents and purposes fit at the end of three weeks.

'On my return I entered Mrs Cluttonhole's basement for the first time; indeed, I entered by the area, and opened the little door under the front steps to give her a surprise. The good woman nearly embraced me.

' "Why, Mr Chard!" she cried, "you're looking better than ever you did."

' "I shall feel better still when I've had a talk with you," said I, following her into the sitting-room. "You've got to tell me something, and no nonsense. Now, Mrs Cluttonhole, put your hand on your heart and swear by all your gods to tell me the truth. Who is that girl in blue who used to come and see me while I was ill, and is she still in the house?"

'She looked at me abashed.

' "Well, Mr Chard, you're your own self again, so there's no 'arm in me tellin' you the truth. To please the doctor and the nurse I 'ad to make up that yam about her bein' Miss Smith who'd just gone away on tour."

' "I don't care what yam you made up. Who is she and where is she?"

' "She isn't anybody, and she isn't nowhere. Oh, Mr Chard, don't be angry. You imagined 'er. She was part of the delirium. But the doctor said as I'd better pretend—"

' "That's not true," I cried angrily. "I saw her long after I was delirious. The last night I was here I saw her. I want the truth, Mrs Cluttonhole, or I shall be very angry with you."

'The poor woman wrung her hands.

' "I've told you the truth. No doubt she seemed real enough—'

'Even as she spoke my gaze wandered to her mantel-piece, and alighted on one of some half-a-dozen photographs.

' "Yes," I interrupted, "she seemed as real as this, and a good deal more real. At least, Mrs Cluttonhole, you've got a photograph of my delirium!"

'And I picked up the photograph and feasted my eyes on it.

'It was my Blue Girl without the least chance of a mistake. I had never seen the photograph before, because this was my first invasion of Mrs Cluttonhole's own apartments.

' "You didn't see 'er," said my landlady, calmly, "because she's dead. She's been dead these five years."

The photograph fell from my hands.

' "She died in the room what you was ill in. A long illness she had, like you, and didn't seem to have no friends. She was a model, and posed for the figure"—yes, I remembered her figure!—"but she was a lady, which is more than you could say for some of them. Good, kind-hearted girl, she was. It fair broke me up when she was taken. Ho, you don't believe me, I see! Well, you wait until Mr Weston, on the ground floor, wakes up, and he'll prove what I say."

'Mrs Cluttonhole obviously did not believe in ghosts, and I—well, I was only just beginning to believe.

'You see, Torrance, I knew so well that I hadn't imagined her, although if I hadn't seen her after the time of my delirium I might have been willing to agree that I had, and to admit, although unwillingly, that the photograph was simply an extraordinary coincidence. But I knew that I had seen her when I was clear-headed and calm.

'So, that, you see, was my first experience of that sort—my seeing a dear and friendly little ghost of a girl, who came to visit and cheer a man who lay friendless and sick in the very room where she had died, and in which she, too, had lain friendless and sick for many weary days and nights. '

A.M. Burrage – The Life And Times.

Alfred McLelland Burrage, better known as simply AM Burrage, was born in Hillingdon, Middlesex on July 1st, 1889, to Alfred Sherrington Burrage and Mary E. Burrage. On his Father's side writing already ran in the family's blood as both he and an uncle, Edwin Harcourt Burrage, were writers of the then very popular boys' magazine fiction.

Life in late Victorian times was by no means easy and writing has always been a precarious career for most. For an insight into the young AM and his surroundings it is interesting to see how certain facts were captured in the 1891 census when he was aged one. The family is listed as living at Uxbridge Common in Hillingdon. His father is 40 and his mother 36. In the next census of 1901, and with it the end of the Victorian era, the family has moved to 1 Park Villa, Newbury. In that time his father has aged 17 years his mother 6 years and young AM has disappeared from the records. It's almost a precursor to one of his stories.

There is little documented about his growing up and education. What we can glean though is something about his environment. His neighbours were varied: a tailor's journeyman, a corn porter, a lodging-house keeper and a grocer's assistant. Nothing particularly illustrious, so times cannot have been as rosy as they should, especially in the light of his Father's hard work. Alfred Sherrington wrote for The Boy's World, Our Boys' Paper, The Boys of England, and various others. He also appears to have written under the pseudonym Philander Jackson and edited The Boys' Standard and that one of his more celebrated pieces was a retelling of the story of Sweeney Todd entitled "The String of Peals; or, Passages from the Life of Sweeney Todd, the Demon Barber".

Sadly Alfred Sherrington Burrage died in 1906. There is a biographical note in Lloyd's Magazine, from 1921, which suggests that young Alfred McLelland was studying at St. Augustine's, the Catholic Foundation School in Ramsgate, and most probably away from home at the time.

A.M. Burrage was 16 years old when he had his first story published; the same year as his father's death, in the prestigious boys' paper, Chums. It was a great start to his professional career and whether doors had been opened by his father and family or not the young man's career now had to stand on its own. He was now primary provider for the household and this was the only way he could do it. His Mother, sister and aunt must be provided for.

Magazine fiction was his family's blood and business and for A. M. Burrage, business was good. He established himself as a competent and creative writer and was busy writing stories and articles on a weekly basis for publications such as Boys' Friend Weekly, Boys' Herald, Comic Life, Vanguard, Dreadnought, Triumph Library Cheer Boys Cheer, and Gem, under the pseudonym 'Cooee'.

However, unlike his father and uncle who had remained firmly and easily categorised as boys' writers, he had his sights set on the more well regarded, more lucrative, adult market. Burrage was aided in his early years as a professional writer by Isobel Thorne of the off-Fleet Street publishing firm Shurey's. Her publications have been characterised as "low in price, modest in payments, but whose readers were avid for romance, thrills, sensation, strong characterisation and neat plotting", and this estimation of her publications also fits nicely the description of Burrage's own writing at that time. For a young writer this sort of readership was vital, and the modest wages he received were bolstered by the exposure the publications brought him. Burrage was certainly helped by Thorne's use of young writers.

At the time Burrage was beginning to really establish himself as a writer, the entire magazine fiction scene was benefiting from what we would now see as disruptive influences: new printing techniques, a growing readership with more disposable income and leisure time and other media failing to provide – though obviously movies and such were only in their infancy at the time. The market was lively and commercial, and the readership interested, excitable and willing to pay. P. G. Wodehouse, of Jeeves fame, recalls these years:

We might get turned down by the Strand, but there was always the hope of landing with Nash's, the Story-teller, the London, the Royal, the Red, the Yellow, Cassell's, the New, the Novel, the Grand, the Pall Mall, and the Windsor, not to mention Blackwood's, Cornhill, Chambers's and probably about a dozen more I've forgotten.

With War clouds darkening the skies of Europe in 1914 Burrage was firmly established as a magazine writer, securing publication in London Magazine and The Storyteller, which were both highly prestigious publications. Alongside he had plenty printed in less illustrious publications such as Short Stories Illustrated.

By now Burrage, a young man of twenty-four-year-was eligible for the Armed Services. Under the 'Derby Scheme' he confirmed that he was available for service if called upon in December 1915. Conscription was to follow shortly though, by that time, Burrage had already voluntarily enrolled in the Artists Rifles.

The significance of Burrage's decision to join the Artists Rifles is made clear by the nature of the unit itself. They formed in the middle of the nineteenth century, a group of volunteer artists comprising musicians, writers, painters and engravers. Minerva and Mars were their patrons, one of wisdom, arts, and defence, the other of war. The unit boasted several significant figures as ex-servicemen, including Dante Gabriel Rossetti, Algernon Charles Swinburne and William Morris. It was a popular unit with students and recent postgraduates, and the training was considered and extensive.

In Burrage's vivid, celebrated account of World War I entitled War is War, he insists that he was a volunteer and not a conscript, though as has already been noted, it is quite possible that his decision to join such a respected territorial unit may have been more of an effort to secure himself a more congenial army posting; had he waited for conscription, he would have had little choice over those with whom he was posted. Unlike poets Wilfred Owen or Edward Thomas, Burrage did not achieve a commission, and he suggests in War is War that this may be a result of his extremely unmilitary personality and his shortcomings as a soldier.

Add to this the fact that as the breadwinner for the family he was putting himself in harm's way. If anything were to happen to him the result on the family would be devastating. With the death of
Edwin Harcourt Burrage in 1916 it came even more starkly into focus.

Even though he was now a soldier he was still a writer and writers had to write. It also helped that it was a distraction from the mindless carnage around him. He experimented with various genres, excelling in the one that was to prove most lucrative for him; the light romance, in which a male character invariably meets a female character, there is a problem or hurdle to their being together, they overcome it and they live happily ever after. Burrage's talent for this formula was such that he could work seemingly endless minor variations from the same basic storyline and so he was able to keep writing a steady body of easy work.

He gives a fascinating account of the practicalities of writing such fiction during wartime in War is War, in which he remarks on the difficulties of censorship: "the problem of censorship was an acute one to me. It was well enough to write a story, but the difficulty was to get it censored. Officers were shy of tackling five thousand words or so, written in indelible pencil..." After some time he managed to find a chaplain who was willing to undertake the censorship. However, in order to secure this chaplain's favour and thus his services he was obliged to appear to be holy. Though he did so in earnest while he was with the chaplain, his efforts were dashed when the chaplain found him, sprawled on top of a young girl, and realised Burrage's piety to be a fraudulent con. As Burrage had anticipated, the reality of his behaviour ensured that this particular opportunity was swiftly ended. Resourceful to the last, though, he writes of his solution: "there were 'green envelopes' which could be sent away sealed and were liable only to censorship at the base, but these were only sparingly issued... I met an A.S.C. lorry driver who had stolen enough green envelopes to last me for the rest of the war; and since he only wanted two francs for them I was free of the censorship from that day forward."

Although we know that Burrage had his family to support at home as an incentive to keep writing, at times in War is War he reveals a more intimate aspect of his relationship with his work.

"It was a great relief to me to write when it was at all possible – to sit down and lose myself in that pleasant old world I used to know and pretend to myself that there never had been a war. Some of my editors seemed of the opinion that we were not suffering from one now. One used to write to me saying "Couldn't you let me have one of your light, charming love stories of country house life by next Thursday." I would get these letters in the trenches during the usual 'morning hate' when my fingers were too numb to hold a pencil, when I was worn out with work and sleeplessness, and when I was extremely doubtful if there ever would be another Thursday".

Writing is a useful therapy and for Burrage it provided a means to escape if only for a short time to a world that he could control and move at will. With the misery and harsh conditions of the War dragging on he was eventually invalided and so he returned to England.

One of the best insights we have as to the character which Burrage presented on his return from the war is to be found in Lloyd's's 1920 publication of Captain Dorry, one of Burrage's story series. In that publication there was included a brief sketch of Burrage, describing his personality.

A.M. BURRAGE is the type of young man who might very well walk out of one of his own stories. He commenced yarn-spinning as a boy of fifteen at St Augustine's, Ramsgate, writing stories of school life to provide himself with pocket-money. Since then he has won his spurs as one of the most popular of magazine writers. Everything he does has charm and reflects his own romantic spirit – for he is incurably romantic and hopelessly lazy. It is his misfortune, although he would not admit it, that his work finds a too ready market. Nevertheless, his friends hope that one day he will wake up and do justice to himself. Otherwise he may end up as a "best-seller", a fate which doubtless he contemplates with equanimity.

Despite the sketch's fairly accurate but negative summation of Burrage's literary output up to that point, some of his stories seem to exhibit a desire to write about more than just his usual romantic plots. The most immediate change of this nature is in his decision to bring some of his wartime experience into his work, despite being perfectly aware that such writing was not at all what his editors desired, for they feared it would upset and intimidate their readership.

An example of this can be found in "A Town of Memories", published in 1919 in Grand Magazine, in which he uses his well rehearsed romantic story with a slight shift of emphasis to explore his own return from the war and the general reception which soldiers received on their return. Following a young officer as he returns to the town in which he grew up, Burrage portrays an almost hostile environment into which he returns; he is unrecognised, and nobody pays any interest, respect or attention to him or his stories of the war, nor even to his reception of the Distinguished Service Order. Instead, the people of the town have their own interests and priorities with which to concern themselves. Though this contentious portrayal of post-war society certainly marks a slight shift in Burrage's writing, he returns to the romantic convention expected of him by reuniting the officer with a beautiful girl who had admired him throughout school. It would be harsh to not accept that market conditions expected one thing and to ignore them would mean turning his back on publications who still clamoured for his penmanship.

Another of Burrage's alternative directions is to be found in "The Recurring Tragedy", in which a General whose war tactics of attrition had been to the slaughtered cost of his soldiers, and he comes to re-imagine his own past as a Judas figure in a terrible vision. The Strange Career of Captain Dorry became a series for Lloyd's Magazine in 1920 about a gentleman crook and an ex-officer with a Military Cross who, idle in peacetime, meets a mysterious man called Fewgin whose business is in stolen goods and mind reading. Fewgin realises Dorry is a suitable candidate for recruitment into his gang of like-minded ex-military thieves, stealing only from "certain vampires who made money out of the war, and, by keeping up prices, are continuing to make money out of the peace". Again, in this motive, we see a glimpse of Burrage's own feelings on the war, as there is undoubtedly a bitterness towards those profiting from the suffering of others in such a manner. Fewgin justifies himself, saying:

"I help brave men who cannot help themselves. I give them a chance to get back a little of their own from the men who battened and fattened on them, who helped to starve their dependents while they were fighting, who smoked fat cigars in the haunts of their betters, and hoped the war might never end."

Burrage began to see slightly more success in the 1920s, achieving a couple of hard back publications entitled Some Ghost Stories and Poor Dear Esme. The latter, a comedy, concerns a boy who, for various reasons, is forced to disguise himself as a girl. Though these hard cover publications were a notable achievement, and one of which he was proud, the fact was that there was less money in it than in the magazines. In his history of the Strand Magazine, Reginald Pound portrays Burrage around this time, likening him to his equally prolific contemporary Herbert Shaw, considering them "two Bohemian temperaments that suffused and at times confused gifts from which more was expected than come forth. They had a precise knowledge of the popular short story as the product of calculated design. Both privately despised it, though it was their living."

The early 1920s, and with them a boom in prosperity, hope and happiness, now brought with them an increase in demand for war stories. Rather than preferring to ignore the atrocities of the war, which had seemed the general attitude in the immediate post-war years, society became more interested and concerned with the manner in which the war was fought, and the greed and political battles which had necessitated such bloodshed. Burrage answered this demand in 1930 with his own epochal piece, War Is War. He published under the pseudonym 'Ex-Private X', saying "were it otherwise I could not tell the truth about myself", though its publisher, Victor Gollancz, "who published the book and greatly admired it, had to point out that the critics would hardly take the book seriously if it became known that the author earned his living producing two or three slushy love stories a week".

In one of a series of letters he wrote to his contemporary and fellow writer Dorothy Sayers, Burrage bemoans how War is War "promised to be a great success, but was only a moderate one". The book itself was received with reviews on both sides of the spectrum. Cyril Fall's War Books, a survey of post-war writing published in 1930, gives a clear indication as to why the critics were so mixed in reception of the book. He writes:

This book is extremely uneven in quality. The account of the attack at Paschendaele and of conditions at Cambrai after the great German counter-attack are very good indeed; in fact among the best of their kind. But the rest is disfigured by an unreasoned and unpleasant attack on superiors and all troops other than those of the front line, which is all the more astonishing because the author is inclined to harp upon his social position as compared with that of many of the officers with whom he came in contact. He does not use as much bad language as many writers on the War, but his methods of abuse will leave on some of his readers at least a worse impression than the most highly-spiced language.

Dorothy Sayers was the editor at Victor Gollanz for anthologies of ghost and horror stories which included stories by Burrage. She says, in one of her letters of Burrage's story The Waxwork, a piece beyond the nerves of the editors, "what you say about "The Waxwork" sounds very exciting, just the sort of thing I want. Our nerves are stronger than those of the editors of periodicals, and we will publish anything, so long as it does not bring us into conflict with the Home Secretary". Though their correspondence began as strictly business, Burrage's acquaintance with Atherton Fleming, Sayers's husband, allowed their interactions to become less formal and friendlier. Burrage wrote of Fleming "I hope to encounter him soon in one of the Fleet Street tea-shops". 'Tea-shop' being a popular euphemism for the pub, where both Burrage and Fleming could frequently be found, though their alcohol consumption came to damage both their health and their professions, with Burrage coming off the worse.

Happily for Burrage, as a result of being featured in one of Sayers's anthologies, The Waxwork became one of his best-known stories and it would grab the attention of the film companies several times down the years even becoming an episode in the TV series 'Alfred Hitchcock Presents'.

The developing friendship between Burrage and Sayers enabled him to reveal more details of his personal life, admitting to her his "neuritis at both ends (legs and eyes)", and hinting at his troubles with alcohol: "Fleet Street is not a good place for a man who delights in succumbing to temptation, and whose doctor says that even small doses of alcohol are poison to him". Sayers sympathises, replying that Fleming "agrees with you entirely about the temptations of Fleet Street; he has, however, succeeded, through sheer strength of character, in being able to drink soda-water in the face of all his fellow journalists".

In another of Burrage's letters, he apologises for a delay in sending proofs of a story, with the words:

I have had a pretty thin time lately through illness and anxiety. And for days on end haven't had the energy in me to write a letter, and when I had the energy to send a complete set of proofs to you I found I hadn't the postage money (This is when you take out your handkerchief and start sobbing). I owed my late agent over £1000, so I got practically nothing out of War is War. He stuck to it. Well, he is paid off now, and so are my arrears of income tax. All this took a toll of my very small earning capacity, and I have been sold up. This on top of something which promised to be a great success and was only a moderate one, was a bit too much for me. Still, in spite of sickness I am resilient and shall float again. "You can't keep a good man down," as the whale said about Jonah.

For a man who had so many stories in so many magazines, and was gaining pace in Sayers's anthologies as a talented writer of horror stories, his income will have been far higher than the then average wage, and yet as he says, he finds himself short of money.

Several questions are left unanswered about his personal life. It is unclear whether he was still supporting family, or whether he spent the majority of his money on alcohol, or whether he chose to conceal his true fortunes from those around him. Perhaps most incongruous is the apparent absence of a wife; though his death certificate indicates that he had one, listed as H.A. Burrage, he seems never to mention her to Sayers.

He was around forty-two when he wrote that apology letter to Sayers, though in tone and circumstance it seems to be from a man in a far later stage of his life.

Burrage continued writing until his death in 1956, and continued to be prolifically published. Indeed, the Evening News alone published some forty of his stories between 1950-56. His death is recorded at Edgware General Hospital on 18th December, and the causes of his death are recorded as congestive cardiac failure, arteriosclerosis and chronic bronchitis. He was sixty-seven years old, and his last address is listed as 105 Vaughan Road, Harrow.

Though his name is not often remembered in lists of prominent writers of his time, or even it's genres, his ghost stories are highly regarded by critics and fans alike, while his life story tells us much about the trials and stresses placed on authors during and after the war, and on soldiers returning from that war. His reluctant acceptance that the money was in the magazines while the esteem was in the poorly-paying hard covers, and his persistence as a writer, speak of a determined man, doomed to circumstance yet living as best he could.

In ending A.M Burrage wrote a few sentences which best sum up two things. Firstly his love for his son Simon (who sadly passed away in October 2013 and was a great and passionate advocate for his Father's works.) and secondly his succinct reasons for writing.

TO JULIAN SIMON FIELD BURRAGE
who at the moment of writing will
soon achieve the great age of four.
From somebody who loves him.

In War is War I admitted being a professional writer, or in other words one who depends for his bread and cheese and beer on writing, typing or dictating strings of sentences which his masters, the Public, are kind enough to buy and presumably to read.

The book brought me letters from a few old friends and a great many new ones. A large percentage of the new friends, who missed having seen that my identity was rather unkindly betrayed by the Press, wrote and asked (a) who I was and (b) what sort of stories did I write?

The answer to the second question will be found in the following pages. The answer to the first question is 'Nobody Much', worse luck.

Most of these stories were written with the intention of giving the reader a pleasant shudder, in the hope that he will take a lighted candle to bed with him—for candle-makers must be considered in these hard times. Some have already made their bow from the pages of the monthly magazines. The best have, quite naturally, been rejected.

www.ingramcontent.com/pod-product-compliance
Lightning Source LLC
Chambersburg PA
CBHW060133260626

47160CB00005B/2094